# Texas Rendezvous

Falling in love with the boss's daughter was just the beginning of trouble for young cowhand Leo Postlewaite.

Exiled from the only home he had ever known, he rides into Denton and into a shoot-out with the infamous outlaw Ignacio McKenna. When Ignacio escapes from custody he rides back to Leo's old haunts and causes trouble for his adopted family.

With Imogen held to ransom and Ignacio's gang causing havoc for his former boss Leo is forced to ride into the outlaw's den and face down his deadly enemy. But will he live?

# Texas Rendezvous

Gary Astill

A Black Horse Western

ROBERT HALE · LONDON

© Gary Astill 2007
First published in Great Britain 2007

ISBN 978-0-7090-8302-3

Robert Hale Limited
Clerkenwell House
Clerkenwell Green
London EC1R 0HT

Typeset by
Derek Doyle & Associates, Shaw Heath
Printed and bound in Great Britain by
Antony Rowe Limited, Wiltshire

# 1

'Get out of my home! You have betrayed my trust!'

Cyrus Breen glared at the young man, his face red with anger.

'Please, Father, I had no thought to be disloyal to you. This was something I could not have foreseen.'

Leo's lean, good looks were somewhat marred by the tightness of his features as he faced the older man.

'I took you under my roof. You were nothing. I raised you as my own son and how do you reward me? – by making love to my daughter. She was your sister for Gawd's sake – a sweet innocent child.'

Cyrus Breen trembled as he tried to keep his anger in check. He was in his fifties with a lean wiry hardness that comes from herding cattle on the back of a cowpony for most of his life. Even though he could number his herds in the thousands he was still not afraid of hard work. He thought nothing of riding with his cowhands and helping out during roundups and cattle drives.

As he confronted the youth standing before him on the ranch-house veranda his hand kept straying to the pistol strapped to his side.

The house itself was a spacious, Spanish-style single-storey building, constructed in brick and stucco. From where the two men faced each other could be seen an extensive walled garden. Mature shrubs and trees vied with arches and patios to make an attractive landscape.

Leo Postlewaite made no move toward his own weapon. He held his hat before him, as if to ward off the anger of his patron, his fingers white with effort as they gripped the rim.

'With due respect, sir, Imogen is not my sister. I know we grew up together but we are not related by blood.'

'You insolent puppy! It's taking all my restraint not to pull this pistol and beat the living daylights out of you. Can you give me reason not to call my crew to tar and feather you for your sneaking, inexcusable behaviour?'

'I'm sorry you feel this way, Mr Breen. It was not my intention to fall in love with Imogen. Nor would I think was it hers to fall for me. It just happened without either of us being aware of what was happening until it was too late.'

'Well, it's not too late for me to throw you off my ranch.'

'I'm sorry you feel that way, Father, but I will leave. I don't want to be the cause of any friction between Imogen and you.'

A female form moved into sight in the garden and was making her way towards the two men on the veranda. The woman was a tall, majestic-looking woman with a full figure. Her light-brown hair hung in long tresses either side of her handsome face. Large gold ear-rings bobbed in time with every step. She was carrying a book that she held folded against her generous bosom.

'What on earth is going on? I was enjoying a quiet read down in the garden when I heard all this shouting.'

'Sorry, my dear, I'm just chucking this serpent off my ranch.'

The woman frowned.

'Serpent? Surely you can't mean Leo!'

She looked with feigned sympathy at the young man.

'I thought he was like a son to you.'

'No longer; I find out he has been deceiving me and making up to my daughter Imogen. You've heard of the serpent in the garden, well, I found one in my house.'

During this exchange Leo stood tight-faced.

'I'm sure he meant no harm, Mr Breen. Imogen is a creature of virtue. I feel confident Leo would not soil that innocence. I know he is a trifle hot-headed but a man living under your own roof would not betray your trust.'

Though her words were supposed to reassure the rancher they conveyed unwelcome images to his imagination. His face got redder.

'I won't have it!' he burst out. 'I've just made it plain he's welcome here no more.' He turned back to Leo. 'You be off my ranch come sundown otherwise I'll horsewhip you.' He turned abruptly from the discomfited Leo. 'Mrs McQueen, shall you take morning coffee with me?'

The woman smiled and advanced up the steps of the veranda.

'It would be a pleasure.'

The couple walked inside and Leo was left to stare after them, his face still tight with the anger he felt at the implications of his good intentions towards his adopted father's daughter.

'Damn!' he muttered after them. 'Damn and damn again!'

Dejectedly he turned and walked slowly down the steps of the veranda and made his way round the side of the house.

The Pentland Ranch had been his home as far back as

he could remember. Taking care he would not encounter Breen again he went up to his room and started packing. He didn't take much – just a few spare clothes and toilet articles that he was able to pack into a small bag.

When he left the house he made his way to the corral and saddled up a dun mare. Despondently he led the beast out and stood looking around him.

'Leo!'

The call brought his head round. A young girl was running from the house towards him. Her long, black hair was flying out behind her as she ran.

'Leo, oh Leo, where are you going?

'Imogen. . . .' He could say no more for she flung herself into his arms.

'Leo,' she said breathlessly, 'tell me it's not true. Mrs McQueen told me you were leaving.'

He sighed dolefully, staring back at her. She had a long oval face with clear olive skin she had inherited from her mother. The whole effect made her into an extremely beautiful young girl. Her large animated eyes stared up at him. Though he was over six feet tall she came up almost to his chin. At last he nodded his head.

'Yeah, Imogen, your pa found out about us and he's chucking me out.'

Her face creased compassionately as she gazed up at him.

'No, Leo, this can't be true. I can't let you go.'

He shrugged helplessly. 'You know I can't go against his wishes after all he has done for me.'

A low sob escaped her as she clung to him.

Inside the house Cyrus Breen sat in the morning-room sipping coffee with his house guest, his mind in turmoil as he contemplated what he had just said to his young protégé, Leo.

When Leo's father had died in his arms he had pledged to care for the dying man's son and now he had banished him. He was beginning to regret his hasty temper but his guest chattered away to him and he was unable to concentrate his mind on the problem.

He had met Victoria McQueen on a trip to Quantock. She was a charming, sophisticated woman, so different from Breen's first wife Jacquenta, a beautiful young Mexican who had died five years ago.

Mrs McQueen exuded warmth and stylish maturity. Cyrus Breen had fallen under her charm. He had invited her to visit him at his ranch and to his great surprise she had accepted readily. She had been at Breen's place for about a month and the rancher was becoming more and more dependent on her for company as his young daughter began to kick over the traces and hanker after a life free from her father's influence.

'Why don't we wander out to the stables and see if that young man you were bawling out has departed yet?' Mrs McQueen said.

On the pretext of powdering her nose she had wandered into Imogen's room and suggested she say goodbye to Leo. Now she wanted to see what would happen when the father caught them together.

'I don't want to see that snake in the grass again,' Breen growled.

'Well, it won't do any harm to watch him go. Come on.'

Suiting words to action Mrs McQueen rose and walked to the door. Cyrus had no option but to follow. So it was that they reached the stables in time to see Imogen with her arms around the young cowboy.

'Damnation, you young whelp,' Breen exploded,

forgetting his manners in his temper. 'I told you to stay away from Imogen!'

'Father, why are you doing this? You can't send Leo away like this. He's as much part of this ranch as you or I.'

'Not any more, he ain't! He's part of nothing here. Now get the hell off my land!'

'I'm going, Mr Breen, right away,' Leo answered.

But Imogen still clung to the young cowboy. Leo gripped her arms and eased her hold on him

'Please, Imogen, we must do what your father wants.'

He swung round and quickly climbed on his saddled mount. With a baffled look at the man who up to that day had been a father to him he tugged the reins and urged his mount towards the gate. He left behind a weeping girl, a self-satisfied older woman and an angry rancher.

As Cyrus Breen watched the young cowboy ride away he had to shrug off a pang of conscience. He raised a hand as if to recall the youngster and then sighed and let him go. His mind scrolled back the years to the time when he and Leo's father had served together in the war. Terry Postlewaite and he had been inseparable friends since childhood and they had signed up together to fight for the South. He remembered their last days together with some pain. The unwanted memories of the Civil War came flooding back to him.

*

There had been very little sleep that night for Major Cyrus Breen and the troops under his command. The day had dawned cold. It was a bitter cold that ate into bones. Men shivered on the cold, hard earth as they tried to sleep. Ghostly phantoms of fog billowed across the meadows that were frosted with a crispy, sugar coating.

'Jesus!'

Breen could hear Captain Postlewaite blaspheming ardently. He peered hard into the fog and could just make out the stone bridge arched over the Potomac River. It was built of sturdy stone and Breen's job was to guard it and not let any of the enemy across. He could see the sentries posted on the river-bank. Some were stomping up and down trying to keep warm while others stood at rest, huddled inside greatcoats in a vain attempt to conserve body heat.

He had only one hundred men with which to do the job but most of them were Texans as was Breen and his captain, Terry Postlewaite.

The fighting had been savage for the last few days with Federal troops swarming all over the farms and meadows of Maryland, trying to surround the Confederate forces ranged against them. Slowly General Gerard's forces were being pushed back till the rebels had eventually formed a bulwark on the line of the river and waited for reinforcements that were being rushed northwards to help hold the line.

How the hell I'm supposed to stop them with only one hundred men, Breen thought despondently.

He had pickets on the other side of the bridge. They were under orders to retreat across the bridge when they sighted the enemy. Only then would Major Breen deploy his men to prevent the enemy forces crossing.

11

He allowed his men to rest. They had fought hard for the last few days, holding the line and only being forced back by the overwhelming numbers of enemy troops that came against them. The accurate shooting of the Texas Brigade mowed down wave after wave of blue-coated soldiers. But still they came on tramping over their fallen comrades and pushing up to be killed. The enemy troops had fought bravely and well. There was no monopoly of bravery on either side.

The Confederates had been pushed back, retreating slowly. Breen had seen his own men being decimated under the constant attacks. Only nightfall had brought a respite from the relentless slaughter. Now after a cold and comfortless night he had to stand and keep the bridge. His orders had been definitive.

'If they get over that bridge, Breen, they can pour reserves in behind our troops and we'll be surrounded. You stop them here, Breen: you stop them dead. To the last man, Breen! To the last man!'

The general had rode away confident in his trust of Major Breen.

He was tempted to rouse the men and ready them for battle but decided to allow them a few minutes more in their cold, uncomfortable billet.

Suddenly he was on his feet and staring towards the bridge. He could sense the change in the men guarding the bridge. They were all of sudden turned towards the river. Their rifles were now pointing to something on the other side.

'Rouse the men, Captain.'

'Rise and shine,' Terry Postlewaite bellowed.

'Not so loud, Captain, you'll waken the enemy. You've heard the old adage, let sleeping dogs lie.'

Postlewaite grinned at his commander. Breen grinned back. The men had known each other since their schooldays and were firm friends. Throughout the war they had served together and knew each other so thoroughly that sometimes the captain anticipated the major's wishes and had the men mustered before Breen voiced his orders.

'Them's not dogs, sir, them's curs to be trashed. And who better to do that than us Texans.'

'Very well, Captain, I want half the men lined up on the river-bank. The other half to hold back in reserve.'

The last few days' fighting had seen Breen's officers thinned out so that only the major and Captain Postlewaite along with a sergeant who had a bullet in his arm remained to command the troops.

Groaning and protesting, the soldiers rose from their cold comfortless beds and were split into two groups – one lot to remain in the bunch of trees as reserve and the second force to take up positions along the river-bank.

Cold and hungry, they began the task of lighting fires in the hope of cooking a meagre breakfast. Leaving his men grumbling and stomping around to get warm Breen walked to the river. The sentries observed his approach and stood to attention.

'Stand easy,' he called out.

He took out his glass and scanned the far side of the river but could make out nothing in the mist.

'You'll be relieved presently,' he said to the guards, 'just as soon as they've had a drink and a cooked breakfast. I think it's fried eggs and flapjacks with molasses and coffee.'

The men grinned their appreciation at the major's little joke. They hadn't had decent food in days. Then they saw the scouts on the other side of the river hurrying to the

13

bridge. When the soldiers reached the bridge they turned and knelt on one knee and waited. Out of the mist came the first skirmishers. Breen's men had orders to not engage the enemy but to fall back across the bridge as the Federal forces advanced.

There was a rattle of muskets sounding sharp and staccato across the water. In good order his pickets retreated back across the bridge loading as they moved. Again they stopped and fired at figures advancing like ghosts through the fog.

Breen turned and waved to his captain and men emerged from the trees and began to trudge across the meadow. The battle for the Aenslow Bridge was about to begin.

Major Breen was proud of the men he had sent across to the other side to give warning of the enemy's approach. They retreated in good order stopping to cover their comrades' retreat and firing back to the far side while they in turn reloaded – each giving the other cover with parade-ground precision. He saw the dark shapes of the advancing forces approach the far side of the river. Then the advance picket were filing past him.

'Well done, men. Go and see if you can scrounge up some breakfast.'

The soldiers nodded at him and continued across the meadow to pass the approaching troops who were to take up where they had left off.

**3**

Captain Terry Postlewaite drew up his men and positioned them in three rows. The first row knelt down and rested gun butts on the earth waiting orders from the two officers. Terry Postlewaite stared across the bridge as he listened to his friend and superior address the men.

'Conserve your ammo, lads. Try and make every shot count. General Gerard gave us this job because we're the best. Success for him depends on the enemy not being able to cross here and hook around behind him. I told him my men will hold and, by God, we shall hold. They will compare our stand here today to that of the Spartans who fought the Persians at Thermopylae. In years to come men will remember us when going into battle. Their war cry will be – Remember the Texans at Aenslow Bridge.'

The first shots were whistling across from the other side.

'Hold your fire! Let them get onto the bridge and then start killing.'

Bullets were coming thicker now as more and more blue-coated soldiers piled onto the bridge.

'First rank fire!'

The kneeling men levelled rifles and fired into the packed ranks of men advancing across the narrow bridge.

'Second rank fire!'

Men were falling on to the stone bridge and their comrades tried to step past them. Breen's men went to their task with deadly accuracy. The opposing ranks were being decimated. Uniform after uniform tumbled to the bridge. The deadly barrage did not go unopposed. Bullets were coming into the Texans and they were taking casualties also. But not so many as they were inflicting, for the advancing soldiers had to clamber over dead and wounded comrades and this did not aid accurate shooting. They could only fire at the far side of the bridge while trying to advance in the face of a deadly hail of lead.

Breen looked at his men quickly and calculated about fifteen were wounded or dead out of his pitiful force of fifty. He was reluctant to call on his reserves so early in the battle but knew there was no option. He signalled Sergeant McKay to advance to the bridge.

By now the oncoming troops were halfway across the bridge. Behind them was a thick carpet of dead and dying soldiers. Officers could be seen behind urging the men on. Breen was proud of his own men as they worked at the business of killing.

Load and fire. Load and fire.

During the battle Breen stood beside his men directing operations. Now he drew his sword and pistol. He knew hand-to-hand fighting was imminent.

'Fix bayonets!' he called, and walked on to the bridge ignoring the bullets whistling over and around him Deliberately he turned his back on the advancing enemy and faced his men.

'Let's give them Yankees a taste of Texas steel.'

He wheeled and ran towards the enemy fully confident his men were following.

Steel met steel as Major Breen parried a bayonet thrust and slashed his blade across the face of the man behind it. There were screams and war cries from his men as they fell upon the enemy.

Breen slashed and thrust his sword and emptied his

revolver into the crowded bridge. Men were screaming and dying as the Texans cut their way forward. Slowly but surely the enemy were giving way under the pressure from Breen's men. The stone on the causeway was slippery with blood and men lay sprawled in obscene postures of death. Boots trampled indiscriminately over dead and wounded. Voices cursed and some prayed or called out for mothers or wives and the killing never ceased. Suddenly the men in front were giving way. Breen sensed the movement.

'Kill!' he screamed. 'Kill the damn Yanks.'

He glimpsed Terry Postlewaite beside him, his sword red with Yankee blood. Captain Postlewaite had his mouth open as he yelled out his battle cry and hacked at the enemy. Breen tripped on a dead soldier and stumbled forward right into the path of a big sergeant. The man grinned devilishly and thrust his bloody blade at Breen. The major twisted and the sergeant's steel entered his shoulder. His sword dropped from suddenly nerveless fingers. The sergeant was triumphant now. He drew back for another strike. Captain Postlewaite flung himself in front of the steel meant for Breen. The bayonet stabbed into his chest but his own blade was slashing a gory wound in the sergeant's throat and the man went down as blood spouted from the death-dealing wound.

Major Breen transferred his sword to his good hand and moved forward. Suddenly there was no more opposition. He blinked in surprise as he saw the blue uniforms fleeing back across the bridge. His men stood and jeered at the fleeing enemy.

'Come back, we ain't finished yet!'

The major had to restrain his men from pursuing the retreating enemy.

'Hold your positions!' he yelled.

17

The men steadied.

'Carry back our wounded. Collect weapons and ammo. We're gonna need them.'

Breen searched for his friend amongst along the blood-drenched bridge. Terry Postlewaite was lying propped against the side of the bridge.

'You men carry the captain.'

They laid him in the meadow. The front of his uniform was saturated in blood. Cyrus Breen knelt beside his friend and began to unfasten the jacket. Postlewaite's eyes opened.

'Don't bother, Cyrus. Look after yourself. I ain't gonna last.'

'Terry, you goddamn took that steel for me. That sergeant had me spiked. Why'd you do it?'

The captain gave a weak smile. 'That's what friends are for, ain't it?'

He convulsed suddenly and blood dribbled from the corner of his mouth.

'Terry!' There were tears in the major's eyes. 'You can't die on me.'

'Cyrus, promise me one thing: look after Leo. Promise me you'll keep him right.'

'God, you know I will, Terry, we both will.'

But Terry Postlewaite was dead and Cyrus Breen swore he would look after his friend's seven-year-old son, Leo and bring him up right and proper.

Cyrus Breen turned and gazed after Leo but the youngster had vanished into the distance.

'Terry, what have I done? Goddamn it, I had no choice.'

He heard a noise on the veranda and turned to see Mrs McQueen with an arm around a distraught Imogen.

'Goddamn it, I had no choice. You would have done the same given my position, Terry.'

**4**

The horse carried him right up the main street before he realized where he was going. With a sudden start, Leo gazed around him, wondering for a moment where he was and how he got here. He hauled on the reins and his mount stopped obediently. Coincidentally they had stopped outside the Black Ace. Leo, with nothing better to do, slid from the saddle and entered the saloon.

The place was the usual hubbub of noise and activity. Drinkers lined the bar and the gaming tables were a hive of activity. Leo pushed his way through to the bar. It was some minutes before the barkeep could serve him and he ordered a whiskey.

'Leave the bottle.'

Morosely he put his elbows on the bar and supped at the harsh liquor while contemplating his future.

He could remember no other life than that at Pentland Ranch. Cyrus Breen was a father to him and now the man had turned against him and kicked him off the ranch. But the greatest loss was Imogen.

In spite of Breen's suspicions the relationship had been completely innocent. Falling for Imogen had been a gradual process. He had hardly known he was in love till that day they had gone riding as they had done dozens of times.

Imogen would pack a picnic and they would head out into the country. Then had come the kiss and everything had changed – one innocent and brotherly kiss! Leo sighed and a hand slapped heavily on to his back. Leo turned with irritation welling up in him.

'Leo, what a piece of luck running into you.'

Broderick Pearson, his friend and drinking partner stood grinning at Leo. Broderick had a face that would have been handsome but for the fact that his chin let him down. Well-spaced blue eyes above a straight nose and a wide, good-humoured mouth were all assets that would have made him good-looking and then – that almost non-existent chin spoiled the perfection of his looks.

'Am I glad to see you! You can help me get this green-horn back to the ranch.'

Without waiting for his friend's reply Broderick grabbed him by the arm and was dragging him into the body of the saloon in the direction of the gambling tables.

'Mr Breen sent me into town to meet the stage and bring Mrs McQueen's son Claude back to the ranch. I met him all right but he wanted to see some action. So he comes in here and begins to strut and blab his mouth off. I can't get him outa the place. Maybe you can persuade him.'

Broderick was rattling on about the awkward cuss he had to deal with. In the end Leo was forced to grab his friend and swing him round to face him.

'Broderick, I ain't going back to the ranch. . . .'

Before he could explain further someone took hold of him by the shoulder and pulled him off-balance. A meaty fist smashed into his nose and Leo saw stars as he tumbled backwards and went down into the sawdust. He looked up to see a hulking young man with a brutish face staring down at him.

'Don't you mess with my friend Broderick,' he warned Leo, in a voice thick with drink.

'Goddamn, I'm gonna punch you into the next town for that, you asshole!'

Leo was on his feet in an instant and swung a round-house at his attacker. The punch connected with the man's ear and he staggered sideways. Leo was after him like a tiger swinging punch after punch and driving the man back with each blow. So furious was his assault that his opponent was helpless to defend himself – never mind retaliate.

A red fury descended on Leo. The man he was attacking was unfortunate in that Leo's tolerance snapped and he happened to be the one who became the victim of the frustration that had been boiling up in him since his confrontation with Cyrus Breen.

'For Gawd's sake, Leo,' Broderick was calling frantically to him. 'He's a guest at the ranch, for Gawd's sake!'

The red haze of anger dissipated. Leo stood swaying slightly as he stared breathlessly at the man he had been battering. Claude McQueen's face was a mess. Blood leaked from his nose and lips. His coarse, thick face was a mass of reddened abrasions and smeared blood. Leo dropped his hands.

'Don't ever hit me again, fella,' he said and turned back to the bar.

Broderick was staring past him with a horrified look on his face.

'Jeez, Leo, what am I gonna tell his ma?'

Then Leo saw his friend's eyes widen and change as he stared past him.

'No, Claude, no. . . !'

Leo swung round and pulled his sidearm as he moved. He saw the gun in Claude's fist and he fired instinctively. The bullet caught the battered man in the gun arm and he spun away, his pistol dropping from his hand. He screamed then. It was just like a woman would scream.

'I'm shot! The bastard shot me! Help me!'

The only man to move to the aid of the screaming man was Broderick. A space had been cleared around Leo and Claude as they had fought. Now the crowd looked on with some interest at the little drama. A fight – a shootout – it was a sideshow to be enjoyed.

Leo slowly holstered his iron.

'It ain't nothing, Claude,' Broderick tried to reassure the wounded man. 'Just nicked your arm. I'll take you to the sawbones. He'll patch you up and stop the bleeding. That was sure a fool play to pull a gun on Leo.'

'Fetch the sheriff. I want him arrested. He's a killer.'

'Damnit, Claude, everyone seen you pull that gun when Leo's back was turned. If Leo was a killer as you say he was you'd be dead right now and no one would have blamed Leo. He was only defending himself.'

'You're on his side. All you cowboys are the same. You'll gang up on me because I'm from back East.'

Casting a disgusted glance at Leo, Broderick began to drag the protesting Claude from the saloon.

Leo sighed. What had promised to be a *helluva* day had turned out as promised. Despondently he turned to the bar and poured himself another generous measure of whiskey.

He realized whatever chance he had of making it up with Cyrus Breen had been seriously jeopardized. After this fight with Claude McQueen, the rancher would have every excuse to brand him a troublemaker. It would take a lot of explaining why Leo had beaten up Breen's house guest and then shot him.

Leo walked out to the hitching rail and mounted his horse. There was no turning back now. He had to ride out before Breen used his influence to have him thrown in jail for a fight he had been forced into.

# 5

'That goddamn tramp picked a fight with you!'

Cyrus Breen's face was livid with anger as he regarded the bruised face of his guest.

The hulking figure of Claude McQueen stood before the rancher, his hat in his hand, looking surly and bitter as he told of the vicious and unprovoked attack on his person.

'He came at me from behind and clubbed me. Must have used his pistol or some such weapon. I didn't stand a chance. While I was helpless on the floor he did this to me.'

Claude indicated his battered face.

'Kicked the living daylights out of me. Then he went for his gun but I was faster. I just shot over his head to warn him off. I didn't want to hurt anyone. But he was shooting to kill. Lucky for me my shot put him off and his bullet only winged my gun arm. In spite of being wounded I fired another warning shot. That scared him some and he turned yellow and ran for it. I could have killed him easy, but I didn't want any blood on my hands. But that Leo

Postlewaite, he was on the prod. He might have killed someone only I chased him off. I guess he picked the wrong fella to mess with.'

'Oh my darling boy.' Victoria McQueen fussed over her son. 'What a dreadful welcome to the Western life.' She turned to Breen. 'You did well to get rid of that Leo. I know you were having some reservations about throwing that troublemaker off your ranch. This should set your conscience at rest.'

'It sure does!' Breen shook his head in regretfully. 'A viper! I harboured a viper in my home. His father was my best friend. During the war he gave his life protecting me from a Yankee bayonet. How could his son have turned out such a wrong 'un.

'Hell, I'm going into town and have the sheriff swear out a warrant for Postlewaite's arrest. He ain't getting away with this. I'll see him in prison, I will. He'll learn he can't thumb his nose at Cyrus Breen. I can't believe the boy I treated as a son could turn out so wayward.'

'You do that, Cyrus. He should be punished for trying to murder my son. Oh, Claude, my poor brave boy, standing up to that killer.'

Victoria McQueen hovered protectively around her son.

'Mrs McQueen, I sure am grateful to you for bringing me out to see my daughter and that snake together. You done me a real good turn exposing that sidewinder. I'm getting so mad I wanna go after that varmint myself. If I ever come across him again I'll shoot him down like I would a mad dog, for that's what he's turned into – a crazy mad varmint!'

In a different part of the house another interview was

taking place. Imogen Breen anxiously questioned Leo's friend, Broderick Pearson.

'You saw Leo in town. Oh, Broderick, how was he? Did he seem sad?'

'Sure Miss Imogen, he looked pretty miserable. But then that new fella, as is Mrs McQueen's son, what Mr Breen sent me in to fetch, he went and picked a fight with Leo.'

'Oh no!' Imogen's hand flew to her mouth. 'My poor Leo, is he hurt?'

'Hell no, miss, begging your pardon. Claude picked the wrong fella to fight. He musta caught Leo on a raw nerve for he laid into that Claude McQueen as if he had a lot o' bile to get out of his system. He knocked seven shades of hell outa that loudmouth braggart. Then when Leo was finished with him he turned his back on McQueen and that's when that sidewinder went for his iron. I sure as hell don't know how Leo did it but he seemed to sense the danger for he whirled slicker than greased lightning and shot a chunk outa Claude's arm. That sure put the fighting outa that bag of wind. He squealed like a stuck pig. Sure thought he was gonna die from that little nick in his arm. I know for a fact Leo could have drilled him centre. Him and I practise a bit together and he sure is fast and accurate. But he only shot to wing that dude.' Broderick shook his head in exasperation. 'He's sure one big bag of wind, that Claude. But what's this I hear about your pa chasing Leo off Pentland?'

'Oh, Broderick, Pa found out that Leo was sweet on me and got real angry about it. Now he's banished him and forbids me to have anything to do with him. Broderick, what am I to do?'

'Hell, Miss Imogen, anyone with half an eye could see

that you and Leo were sweet on each other. The only ones what didn't know were the ones involved – you and Leo and, I suppose, Mr Breen.

'I didn't have time to find out what Leo's plans were 'cause I had to drag that intolerable hog to the sawbones. By the time I came back to the saloon Leo was gone.' He shrugged helplessly. 'I'm his best friend and if I knew where he was at I'd head on after him. For the life of me I can't think where he'd go. As far as Leo was concerned this was his life. He never hankered after anything else. I guess he figured you and him would get hitched and he'd run the ranch for you.' Broderick sounded as miserable as he looked. 'I'm real sorry, miss. I guess we'll both miss him.'

'Broderick, could we ride out and find him? He means too much to me to let him go off like that.'

The young cowboy stared at the woeful face of the girl and shrugged helplessly.

'I guess we could enquire in town and find out what direction he headed. Then if you were real set on it we could try. But it won't be no easy ride, Miss Imogen. It'll be like a hopeless kinda quest.'

'Broderick, if you would! I can't just let him ride out of my life like that without doing something.'

For a week Leo Postlewaite rode the trails not caring in what direction he was headed. He had become a drifter with no particular aim in mind. On the second day he had stopped at a town for supplies. He could not even remember the name of the place. Coffee was an essential part of a cowboy's menu as well as tobacco and he stocked up on these along with a sack of beans and flour and molasses. His money was plentiful for Cyrus Breen had paid him a regular wage and most of this Leo had saved.

During his meandering he thought long and hard about his situation.

'I guess Cyrus sure is set against me marrying Imogen,' he mused and sighed deeply. 'Hell, maybe I shouldn't have sparked up to Imogen, but I ain't a man of wood. And she sure made me believe she was of the same mind.'

His camp-fire burned brightly and he lay back with his head resting on his saddle and stared up into the night sky.

'I wonder what she's doing right now. Maybe she's forgotten me already. Guess Cyrus has some rich rancher's son lined up to marry his daughter, or even a banker, or some such dude. Hell, I'm just an orphan and everything I ever had came from Cyrus. Damnit though, I worked hard for him – never shirked my load. He admitted himself he couldn'ta done it without me.'

He sighed deeply, feeling loneliness like a slab of undigested meat sitting uncomfortably in his stomach.

'I guess I just gotta forget all that. I'll sign up at the next place I come to that's hiring. Regular work will keep me from feeling so sorry for myself.'

After several days he got tired of his own cooking and determined to call at the next town he came across and treat himself to some home cooking and at the same time enquire about a job. Another factor in his decision was the change in the weather.

From warm, dry days a cold easterly wind started up and

rain clouds scudded in. Before he reached any habitation the rain came down in sudden large blots. Leo shook out his slicker and covered up.

The wind and rain spewed at him in vicious gusts, driving into his horse's face and trying to heave the slicker from his shoulders. He let the horse find its own way and tried to hunch down deeper inside his slicker. The rain increased in volume and he could see the spray bouncing from the folds of his waterproofs. The noise of raindrops battering at him obliterated all other sounds. Then he saw the sign. Through the downpour he could make out the name – Denton.

'Any port in a storm,' he muttered.

The horse found the road although it was awash with rainwater and followed it. Rain-filled ruts made the going treacherous but Leo trusted his mount to keep them both safe. Buildings loomed out of the murk. He kept going past huddled dwellings and warehouses. Intermittent lamplight broke up the gloom as he rode till he came to what appeared to be the wide main street of the town.

Peering through the deluge he was on the look out for a café. Then he saw the livery stable and decided to put his horse under shelter. If he were to stay any length of time in this town then he would need a dry rig when he finally decided to ride on.

The stable hand came out from the back when Leo rode his horse in through the big double doors. He was glad of the respite from the relentless pounding of the rain.

'Howdy,' he greeted a young fellow with vacant-looking eyes, and got a nod in return. 'Need stabling, feed and water.'

'Sure, sure.'

'Will you off-saddle and stow my things?'

'Sure, sure.'

Leo slid wearily from the horse. The animal stood with head down – battered by the storm, as was its rider. While keeping his slicker on he shook it to remove some of the surplus water.

'Where can a fella get a meal and a drink around here?'

The stable hand stared into the distance and Leo could see his lips move as he silently repeated the question. He turned those disconcertingly vacant eyes on Leo before replying.

'Silver Penny.'

The words were enunciated slowly. The youth's mouth moved as if chewing them before allowing the sounds to pass his lips.

'Which direction?'

Leo had to stop himself from imitating the youth's method of articulation, not out of a sense of mockery but because this was the first person he had spoken to in more than a week and the concept of speaking slowly was infectious.

The youth pointed and then as if he had completely forgotten his customer he took the horse's reins and guided the animal to a stall.

Leo found the Silver Penny about five buildings down the street. He stepped inside the saloon and dripped all over the sawdust as he walked to the bar.

The place was crowded with people sheltering from the rain. A tall, fat man, wearing a set of handlebar moustaches and a crisp clean apron was serving. Everything about the man was immaculate – well-groomed hair and tidy moustache along with scrubbed hands and clean fingernails.

'Howdy, can I have a drink and a meal?'

'Sure thing.'

The fat man reached up and rung a large brass bell.

'I do the drink. My brother'll get your meal.'

'Beer.'

Another fat man waddled into the room and approached Leo. Where the barkeep was tidy his brother was filthy. The contrast was disconcerting.

Unwashed hair straggled in lank strands on to a grimy shirt collar. The man had shaved earlier in the day but missed parts and unsightly tufts of hair grew like isolated stands of prairie grass on his fat sweaty face. His apron was greasy and globules of food were smeared in places. The unpleasant odour of a man unfamiliar with a bathtub wafted into Leo's nostrils.

'What can I get you, cowboy?'

Leo sighed. He was reluctant to take anything from this man's kitchen but now he was committed he decided that to refuse would be churlish.

'What about hot cakes?'

The man nodded. 'I do hot cakes that melt in your mouth. What you want with them?'

'Maple syrup?' Leo asked without much hope.

He was sick of molasses and the thought of maple syrup made his taste buds water.

The fat neck wobbled as the man nodded again.

'Good choice, I got maple syrup. You grab a seat. You won't have to wait long. I just made a fresh batch of dough.'

Leo took his beer to a vacant table and removed his slicker while he waited for the hot cakes with some misgivings.

The cook's boast was as good as he made out and the

heaped plate of cakes smothered in maple syrup disappeared as fast as Leo could push them in.

'Goddamn best batch of hot cakes I ever ate,' he declared fervently when he went to the bar for a whiskey to chase down the meal.

'Archie is a right filthy bastard, but he's the best cook in Texas,' his brother boasted as he served Leo.

Leo grinned wryly and thought that about summed up the cook.

The staccato sound of gunshots sounded as if they were right outside the saloon. Every head turned to the doorway and a hush fell over the crowd.

## 7

More gunshots sounded and then there was a concerted rush to the doors. As they crowded round the opening those in the forefront were pushed outside by the pressure of men anxiously craning to see the cause of the gunfire. Leo followed and was caught up in the crush of men around the doorway. Like a reluctant swell of cattle the men spilled onto the boardwalk and then stopped as they took in the scene in the street.

The rain had eased off to a slight drizzle. Nightfall was an hour or so away but the cloud and rain cast a gloom in the street. The murky shapes of horsemen could be seen outlined in the lightly falling rain. There were half-a-dozen riders and they formed a circle around a burly man standing hatless in the rain. He was clasping a hand to his

31

arm and blood leaked on to his shirtsleeve. Near him lay a body. By the body lay a shotgun. Leo saw the glint of a metal star on the vest of the injured man.

The lawman's face was tight drawn as he held his wounded arm. He was a big man with a full-grown beard covering the lower half of his face. His eyes were wide-spaced above a long straight nose. Even though he was in pain and the horsemen had their weapons trained on him he stood defiantly in the rain without a trace of fear on his face. As the men from the saloon spilled outside some of the riders turned their pistols towards them.

'None of you gents interfere in this and you won't get hurt,' one of the gunmen called out.

Some of the onlookers began to shove back again. No one wanted to get involved in the fracas.

'Sheriff, you want to say anything before I blast you to hell?'

Like the rest of the riders in the group the speaker was wearing a slicker and his hat had taken so much moisture that the brim drooped down hiding most of his face.

'Ignacio, you're one murdering sonofabitch. You may blast me, but your days are numbered. My only regret is I won't be there to watch you swing on the end of a rope.'

The sheriff turned his head towards the men watching from the boardwalk.

'You men there grab a piece and blast these sonsof-bitches to smithereens. I'm deputizing you all.'

For answer the leader of the group turned his pistol and thumbed two shots over the heads of the onlookers. The crowd of men on the boardwalk flinched and those at the back stumbled back into the saloon. The rest were caught where they were standing, most afraid to move in case they attracted the gunmen's attention.

32

'If any of you wanna piece of the action I can tell you now there won't be anyone left standing by the time we finish shooting.'

As the men edged back Leo found himself to the forefront of the crowd. He stood gaping at the riders in the rain but mostly his eyes were on the leader of the group.

'He can't get you all,' called the sheriff. 'Gun the bastards down.'

The man who had done all the threatening laughed. It was a harsh sound in the still damp air.

'Sheriff, these people pay you to protect them. Nobody pays them to get killed. OK, boys, anyone as much as twitches over there let loose with everything. I want that boardwalk swimming in blood.'

Not a man moved. Leo stared at the group and his hand had strayed to his holstered Colt. He didn't know what he intended doing but he knew he couldn't stand by and watch the lawman be gunned down without doing something about it. He waited and watched. The outlaw raised his pistol and at the same time Leo had his Colt in his hand.

The first shot went low and hit the horse causing it to leap sideways. Whether he did this deliberately from a reluctance to shoot a man without warning Leo did not know. In any case all hell broke loose.

The lawman dropped to his knees and scooped up the shotgun. Most of the gunmen were turned towards Leo and trying to aim at him from the top of plunging horses. The squeals of the horse wounded by Leo's shot spooked the rest of the animals and they bucked and spun around. The riders were attempting to shoot towards the gunman on the boardwalk and control their horses at the same time.

Leo kept firing into the group of riders. He saw one topple from the saddle while another clutched at a shoulder and leant over the neck of his mount. The sudden roar of the shotgun was a mini explosion of sound in the street. A rider was plucked from the top of his horse. He thudded into the street sending splashes of muddy water into the air. In a few frantic moments the raiders found the tables turned on them. They were wrenching at reins trying to turn their mounts to get away from the danger. Leo held his fire as he saw the gunmen were breaking away from the confrontation. The sheriff let fly with his second barrel but it seemed to have no more effect than make the fleeing horsemen go that much faster.

Colt in hand Leo ran out into the street. The wounded lawman had placed the butt of his shotgun in the mud and was leaning on the weapon.

'You hurt bad, Sheriff?'

Cool blue eyes were turned on Leo. A faint smile twitched into place.

'You the fella as started the shooting?'

Leo shrugged. 'I couldn't think of anything else to do. There was so many people behind me I couldn't get back in the saloon.'

The sheriff's grin widened.

'Youngster, I owe you my life.'

Then his face turned sober again as he regarded the body lying face down in the street.

'Murdering sonsofbitches – killed my deputy.'

His glance took in the two bodies of the fallen raiders.

'Guess two of them in no way makes up for Jake.'

He turned towards the men at the saloon.

'Some of you loafers get on out here and take Jake's body down to the morgue.'

The men seemed reluctant to come forward, perhaps ashamed of their cowardice earlier.

'Pearly, and you, Jones, lend a hand here.'

Thus named, two men detached themselves from the crowd and walked forward. As if wanting to make up for their recalcitrance more figures came behind and plucked the dead gunmen out of the mud.

'You need any help, Sheriff?' Leo asked.

'Sure, son, walk with me down to the sawbones. I'll get this wound attended to and then I guess I can buy you a drink.'

'What, me as deputy! Oh no! You got the wrong fella, Sheriff.'

Sheriff Phil Morgan stared out of steady blue eyes at the youngster who had so fortuitously intervened in the main street of Denton. He liked what he saw. The young man hadn't shaved since he had left Pentland. Leo was growing a beard hoping to alter his appearance and in doing so sever all links with his past life. In spite of looking like a saddle tramp he gazed out at the sheriff with dark hazel eyes that held no guile.

'Tell me, son, where are you heading?'

Morgan winced as the doctor tugged the bandage tight.

'Hell, doc, go easy there. I'll be needing that there arm soon as I can saddle a horse and go after those damn bandits.'

'You ain't going nowhere with that arm for a week or so. I'm putting it in a sling and you gotta give it some rest. No shooting or riding for a while. Just curb your impatience and let someone else set the world to rights. Them fellas as shot you up are long gone towards the border is my guess. You won't catch up with them with a bust arm.'

'Sure, sure, Doc, that's just what I'm counting on. They know they winged me and shot my deputy so they won't expect me to come after them.'

'Hell, why'd I open my mouth?' the doctor said in disgust a and gave the bandage an extra hard tug.

'Damn you, Doc, I won't have no arm left if'n you keep jerking like that. Why the hell you ever took up medicine is sure a mystery to me.'

'I sure wonder at that myself when I gotta patch up moose-heads like you so's they can go out and get themselves shot up again.'

Leo tried to hide a grin as he listened to the doctor and the sheriff. It was obvious they were old acquaintances and in spite of the sentiments expressed had more than uncommon regard for each other.

'And forget that sling, Doc. I can't have that interfere with my shooting and riding what I aim to do soonest.'

'Well, go and get your damn fool head blowed off. And when they take you out to Boot Hill I'm going to be there when they're shovelling the dirt on. I'll be yelling, I told you so!'

'Well, long's I won't be able to hear you that'll suit me fine.'

For a moment the two men glared at each other before the sheriff slid down off the couch where he had perched while the doctor worked on him.

'What do I owe you for the treatment, and next time I

come here less of the jaw-ache or I might just change my doctor?'

'Hell, Phil, you owe me a drink and I guess you owe that young fella a drink and then some from what I can make out.'

The doctor turned a critical eye on Leo.

'Take my advice, don't let Morgan talk you into putting on a deputy's badge. If'n you take a walk up to Boot Hill there's a whole row of graves there called Deputies Hallow. He wears out deputies faster than a whore wears out her knickers.'

He turned to his instruments and began to tidy them away.

'Go on the pair of you. I'll see you down there.'

When Sheriff Morgan and Leo walked into the Silver Penny men crowded up eager to buy them both a drink. The sheriff waved them away with some good-natured bantering. As soon as they were alone the lawman began to quiz Leo.

'Where you heading, kid?'

Leo pulled a face.

'Nowhere in particular; I guess I was just drifting. Thought to hook up with a cow outfit and do the only thing I know anything about.'

The lawman eyed Leo shrewdly.

'You running from something?'

Leo's eyes clouded momentarily.

'Not so's you'd notice. I ain't put down no roots nowhere yet.'

'I'm serious about you becoming a deputy. Pay's as equal to a cowhand's but you get cartridges and stabling thrown in.'

'Hell, Sheriff, I ain't no lawman.'

'I weren't always a lawman. I herded beef for a time. Then a crowd of rustlers stole some cattle from a friend of mine. Gunned him down in the process. Left him with a widow and two orphan kids. Me and a bunch of fellas took after them rustlers. Caught up with them and in a fight we killed some. The two survivors we hung from a cotton-wood limb. It didn't bring back my pal to his family but them rustlers sure as hell never stole or murdered again. That's what this job is all about. Making the world a safer place for the honest folk. Think about it. First thing in the morning I'm lighting out after that gang. I sure could do with a reliable man at my back when I catch up with that gang.'

'You seem pretty sure you'll find them.'

The lawman gave a grim smile.

'Like I said to Doc, they won't expect me to come after them with a busted arm and no deputy. I reckon on surprising them owlhoots. Don't forget we winged some of them. They'll want to rest up and lick their wounds. I'll sneak up on them and take the whole murdering bunch. They owe me a deputy and I owe my deputy. Anyways, think on my proposition. It ain't the best job in the world, but it sure is a lot easier than herding a bunch of ornery longhorns.'

'Who were them fellas anyways?'

'Mostly Mex bandits. They're led by a fella calls himself Ignacio McKenna – son of an Irish miner and a Mexican gal. He's mean as hell and has been giving us a lot of bother robbing stages and stealing cattle. Jake, my deputy, spotted him and his pals coming into town. One of the big ranchers had a sizeable shipment of beeves to pay for and the bank took delivery of the money. How the hell Ignacio found out about it beats me. I guess every town has its men willing to sell information. It weren't no secret the money was in the bank. It might have been better if poor Jake had never spotted them fellas. As it was we didn't have time to organize a reception committee for them – just Jake and me. I guess I must be getting old to let them get the drop on me like that.'

Sheriff Phil Morgan shrugged his shoulders ruefully. He threw back his drink and nodded to Leo.

'See you in the morning, kid.'

'I ain't said I'd be joining you,' Leo replied.

Sheriff Morgan spotted the doctor arriving. He walked over and together they sat in on a card game. There were three other men in the game. They were dressed in business suits and Leo come to the conclusion this was a regular game played by a group of friends. He ordered another drink and enquired about a room for the night

'That's your mount, Leo, I picked him myself for you. He's got plenty of bottom and will still be there at the end of a hard day's riding. Thought you might want to rest up your own mount.'

Leo looked hard at the sheriff, but he was busy checking his own tack and had his back turned to the youngster.

'I ain't said as I would go with you.'

'I've packed a few beans and flour. Archie sent a bag of fresh baked cookies and a sourdough loaf. Said he kinda took a liking to you on account you praised his hot cakes last night.'

'Hell, Sheriff, I ain't sure I wanna go on this manhunt thing.'

Sheriff Morgan took up the reins and led his mount outside. Leo noticed he was favouring his wounded arm. The lawman swung up on his horse.

'There's a Winchester in the boot and plenty of spare ammunition in the saddle-bags.'

Leo was beginning to get annoyed, but before he could make any kind of protest the sheriff wheeled his mount and looked down at him.

'It stopped raining soon after the raiders lit out of town. With a bit of luck their tracks will be easy to follow. At least we'll know what direction they took. My guess is they headed for the buttes. At least that's what I would do in their shoes. There's canyons enough to hide in.'

The sheriff heeled his mount and moved off. Leo gazed after the rider in exasperation and then with a muttered curse he grabbed the horse the sheriff had saddled for him and led him out of the livery stable. Grumbling under his breath he followed the lawman. His every intention was to come down to the livery and tell Sheriff Morgan he was not cut out to be a lawman. Now in spite of his resolution he found himself following the sheriff like a dutiful subordinate.

'Hell's bells,' he muttered, as he urged the horse after the retreating back of the lawman. 'What am I letting myself in for?'

They found the tracks a few miles out from the town. The hoofs had cut up the trail in the characteristic manner of horses galloping fast through soft going. The mud had held the deep impressions of the hard-riding group and the trail was easy to follow.

'We might have bother when we get to the rocky approach to the buttes. But by then hopefully we'll have a reasonable idea in what direction they'll be heading. No one's ever tracked them before, but then no one's ever shot them up before. That musta come as a bit of a shock to Ignacio. They oughta be pretty demoralized by now. They've lost two of their men as well, which won't make them too happy. Just keep your eyes peeled.'

After that they rode in silence, keeping up an easy canter for most of the morning. At noon they stopped for a bite to eat – sipping water from their canteens and using their knives to carve slices of sourdough.

'Just get used to cold fare,' Morgan advised Leo. 'We can't risk a fire from now on.'

It was not far off nightfall when they found a stream and decided to make camp for the night.

The horses sucked greedily at the fresh water. The men ate more of the sourdough and relished the sugariness of the cookies provided by the cook at the Silver Penny. They washed the meal down with sweet water from the stream. Night was on them as they rolled into their blankets. There was a discernible chill in the air, this close to the mountains.

Leo listened to the night sounds around him. In the last week or so he had grown used to being alone as he fled from his former life. A faint snore reminded him he was not alone. He sighed deeply. And then a sudden thought occurred to him.

The man who had insisted he come on this manhunt seemed determined to drag him along. Sheriff Morgan was obviously a lawman of some experience, while Leo was just a green youth. There must have been dozens of men back in Denton the sheriff could have called upon to join him and yet he had chosen Leo. Just the two of them were to take on a bunch of dangerous outlaws. The more Leo thought about it the more he figured the sheriff must hold him in high regard. With that comforting thought Leo fell asleep.

He dreamed of riding the land with a beautiful, sultry, young woman. In the dream they laughed and flirted and Leo smiled in his sleep as they rode in happy accord.

In the morning after a cold breakfast they saddled up and started out again. Leo yearned for a mug of hot coffee. He recalled his own recent travels as he had fled his former life.

Each morning he would get a fire going and somehow the flickering flames and heat were a comfort to a lonely man. Night had seen him squatting by a blazing fire with hot coffee bubbling in the pot. The fire had given him a feeling of security as well as warmth. Now he was on a manhunt after a bunch of killers without even the basic comforts of a fire and a hot breakfast.

He sighed and again wondered why he was here. Why was he riding on the trail with a man he hardly knew after a gang of ruthless men he did not know at all? But he was beginning to figure out the answer to that question.

There was something heroic about the man he rode with. Yesterday he had seen the courage of Sheriff Phil Morgan as he had stood in the street alone and with his dead deputy lying in the mud.

The lawman had squared up to the gunmen even as he waited for them to gun him down. He fully expected to join his deputy in the mud with a gutful of lead. In spite of that impending fate he had defied the outlaws – taunting them with their own inevitable deaths on the end of a rope. It was that cool courage that had drawn Leo to come to Morgan's aid and he supposed it drew him along on this mad but strangely intriguing venture.

He stared at the man's straight back as he followed behind him. His gaze drifted past his companion and up to the buttes that were their ultimate destination. That was where Morgan expected to find the outlaws. There was nothing to indicate that any other creatures occupied this land.

Right now only the pines and the sky filled with streaky clouds that filtered stippled sunlight over the land were all that occupied Leo's vision. And inevitably he wished the man he was riding with was not a man but a young girl with dark hair and olive skin and a bewitching smile and wondered what she was doing and if he would ever see her again.

# 10

'Of course I know how to run a ranch. I ran a goddamn merchandise store for years. Was boss of ten men. Cattle is just stock and that's what I know.'

This was a lie. Claude was no more than a clerk in a grocery store and had no responsibilities other than keeping the books up to date.

Cyrus Breen looked dubiously at the young, bullnecked man before him. He had some misgivings about giving over charge of the ranch to Claude McQueen.

Previously the disgraced Leo Postlewaite, with Cyrus looking over his shoulder, had done the job. The ranch was so vast Cyrus knew he could not run it without help. Victoria McQueen had suggested her son for the job as foreman even though her boy had no experience with cattle.

'Claude is so smart he'll soon pick up the job. Oh, I'm so happy he's here with me. It makes my family almost complete to have him by me. It means,' she suggested coyly, 'I might be tempted to stay on a little longer.'

'Dang me, Victoria, I'd hate to see you go.'

Cyrus sounded flustered. Indeed, the thought of Mrs McQueen leaving Pentland disturbed him profoundly. He was growing daily more fond of the woman and her company was extremely comforting to him.

Victoria McQueen had made it her ambition to become mistress of Pentland. When she first met Cyrus he was just another ticket to a free holiday. When she accepted his invitation to visit him on his ranch it had been her intention to live off his hospitality till something better offered itself. When she saw the wealth inherent in the ranch, subtly her intentions had altered. That was one of the reasons she had sent for Claude. It was also her reason for fostering the rift between Cyrus and Leo.

Imogen was the key to her plans. As she perceived it the growing relationship between Leo and Imogen had been an obstacle. While she was working on getting rid of Leo she had sent for Claude. Now it was her ambition to throw her son and Imogen together as much as possible and generate a relationship between the two. She reasoned that Imogen, bereft of her lover, would fall easy prey to her charming son.

'All right then,' Cyrus grumbled to a delighted Claude. 'I'd better take you on a tour of the ranch and introduce you to the hands.'

Imogen was tacking up her pony when she saw her father and Claude walking up to the corral. Sandy, the ancient cowhand, too old now to haze cows, was hovering round aching to help his beloved mistress.

'Miss Imogen, you oughta 'low me to saddle up for you.'

The girl grinned mischievously at the old-timer.

'Sandy, I got to learn sometime how to look after myself.'

Which was a complete misrepresentation of Imogen's abilities for she had been riding almost since she could walk.

'You, old man,' Claude called imperiously, as he arrived at the fence, 'saddle me a fine horse. I'm riding out with Mr Breen.'

Sandy looked to Cyrus for conformation of the order. The men of the ranch usually picked and saddled their own mounts. Cyrus looked away, too embarrassed to meet the hostler's eye.

'Hurry, man, don't stand there like a halfwit. I want to go today, not next week sometime.'

Hurriedly Imogen mounted.

'See you, all,' she called, and gigged her mount quickly away, afraid she would say something she would regret.

The atmosphere between her and her father was extremely strained since he had banished Leo. Claude called after her but she affected not to hear.

Soon she was well out of earshot and settled down to a pleasant afternoon ride. Her thoughts were not happy ones for she was remembering her rides with Leo and the good times he and she had together. Since his departure she had racked her brains trying to figure a way to get in touch with him. But Leo had been dismissed so abruptly they had made no provisions to keep in touch.

As she rode out to the north range she saw some of her father's men working the cattle. She turned her mount in that direction and was soon hailed by one of the hands. He spurred his horse towards her. She was pleased to see it was Broderick.

'Howdy, Miss Imogen, I guess you come out especially to see me. I know I'm irresistible to the female race.'

In spite of her dire thoughts regarding Leo she laughed out loud at Broderick's boastfulness.

'Broderick, you are a charming chappie but you know my heart belongs to another.'

The cowboy gazed earnestly at her.

'I sure hope you mean who I think you mean.'

'Oh, Broderick, have you found out where he went?'

'No, miss, I asked all over town but no one saw him leave. But I'm sure he'll write as soon as he's settled. He'll not be able to forget you and he and I are good friends. Leo's not the type to ride off and forget who his friends are.' He paused for a moment before speaking again. 'Is it true that Claude is taking Leo's job?'

'I'm afraid so. Dad told me last night. He's a horrible man. I wish he'd never come here. He makes my flesh creep every time he looks at me. Oh, Broderick, how could everything go so wrong? Do you think Leo is all right? How did he seem to you on that day?'

'I'll not lie to you, Miss Imogen, Leo was all cut up that day. He was as miserable as a preacher on a wet Sunday. Never seen him so down. I wanted to have one last drink with him only I had to take that fool Claude to the sawbones to get his arm patched up. By the time I returned to the saloon Leo had lit out. I sure wish I knew where he was at now, then I could put your mind at rest,

Miss Imogen.'

'Do you think he'll forget us here at Pentland?'

'Nah, not Leo, he'll not forget you, Miss Imogen. Your face is imprinted on Leo Postlewaite's heart.'

'You will let me know if you hear anything, Broderick.'

'Sure, Miss Imogen, you'll be the first to know. For all we know he's bought himself a little spread and is working hard building it up so as he can send for you and you and him will live into a happy old age together.'

Imogen's vision was suddenly blurred with tears. She sniffled and wiped at her eyes.

'Thank you,' she muttered indistinctly, but was unable to continue.

Abruptly she pulled her horse's reins and rode away.

Broderick reached up and scratched his head.

'Now, what did I say that made the little lady cry?'

He gazed in some perplexity after the diminishing figure of the girl till horse and rider faded over the next rise.

# 11

Leo woke and instinctively looked towards the mountain range that Morgan had said was their ultimate destination. Ignacio and his outlaws were out there somewhere licking their wounds and perhaps regretting ever having ventured into Denton.

He could make out the faint grey blur of daylight just becoming visible above the hills. The horse he had hobbled last night shuffled closer to the camp. Leo blinked the sleep from his eyes. His hand closed over the butt of his Colt. Somewhere to the right he heard the slight noise of stone moving on stone. With a quick movement he rolled from his blankets and sat up.

A figure rose up not more than a dozen feet from the sleeping men. Leo had just time to see the long barrel of a rifle before he fired at the shape. The man stumbled backwards as his rifle fired, the bullet going somewhere into the air. Leo heard his companion swear and then he was busy firing as other figures rose up and rushed the camp. They were coming from every direction.

Beside him, Sheriff Morgan opened up with his six-gun. Leo fired point blank into a face. The man was flung backwards into the path of another raider. Both men became entangled with each other and Leo fired again into the mix of bodies. Then his hammer fell on an empty chamber.

Now it was Leo's turn to curse and he scrabbled round for his rifle. Before he could find the weapon another dark figure threw itself on top of him. He felt a stunning blow to the head as the man clubbed him. Frantically Leo grappled with his attacker and more by luck gripped the pistol the man was using to batter him.

As the men struggled to kill each other Leo could hear Morgan still loosing shots at the attackers. Then his whole attention was on the man he wrestled with.

His head was reeling from the blow from the man's pistol. Fingers closed round his throat and Leo choked as his wind was cut off. He drew his knees up underneath and forced his attacker to the side. His assailant was big and powerful and Leo had to extend all his strength to contain him as the man tried to strangle him and free his weapon from the youngster's desperate grip. Again they rolled and the bandit came back on top.

Leo's vision was blurring as he was starved of air. In desperation he drove a fist into the face hovering above him. The man grunted but held his grip on Leo's throat. Leo punched again and felt the nose give under his punch. Again and again he drove his clenched fist into man's busted nose and in the end the punishment was too much and the bandit released his grip.

Never had air tasted so sweet as the young cowboy sucked in breath. But he did not give up his punishing blows to the man's face. In a quick movement the bandit dropped the pistol they had been fighting for and snatched a blade from his belt.

Leo saw the gleam of the steel as the point plunged down towards his neck. He had seen the pistol drop as the bandit abandoned the struggle for possession of the weapon and with a quickness that surprised himself he grabbed the weapon and swiped at the knife.

There was the clash of metal on metal and something sliced along Leo's jaw. Ignoring the sudden shock and pain, he used the pistol to hit the knifeman in the face. The pistol smashed into the man's nose already bloody from Leo's punches. Abruptly the man pulled away and scrabbled to his feet. Leo kicked out and caught the bandit behind the knees as he turned to flee. The man pitched forward and the young cowboy was on him like a cat after an escaping prey.

Still clutching the abandoned pistol he clubbed the man on the back of the head. Twice he brought the weapon down on the feebly struggling bandit and then the man was still.

Wildly, Leo looked around him expecting another

attack but all he could see were shapes fleeing in the emerging light rays from the mountaintops as the sun highlighted the scene.

'Goddamn it, kid, I was fast asleep when you started shooting. Next time give me some warning before you cut loose.'

Leo stared at the sheriff as the man knelt beside him. Morgan was peering out into the distance as he spoke. Slowly the lawman stood.

'Waal, I guess I was wrong about them there bandits,' Sheriff Morgan stated laconically, still staring out from the camp. 'They found us, not the other way round as I had planned.'

For the first time he turned to Leo and looked at the young cowboy.

'You hurt, son? That looks a nasty cut on your face. Were you shaving when they come up on us? Let me look at that.'

The sheriff knelt beside Leo.

'Sure is nasty, that'll need stitching.'

Leo put his hand to his jaw and tenderly explored the cut. He winced as he felt the deep gash along his jawline.

'Let's see if any of these fellas are alive and then I'll tend to that wound.'

Morgan indicated the man lying by Leo.

'That fella you bin getting cosy with dead?'

'Dunno,' Leo mumbled, 'he sure did his best to finish me off.'

Together they rolled the bandit over and Sheriff Morgan whistled.

'Son of a bitch, it's Ignacio himself. Son, you sure are one mean cat when it comes to thwarting this bandit chief. First you chase him and his gang out of town, and today you club him into surrender. This'll bring you in a goodly reward.'

Within moments the handcuffs were on the still uncon-scious Ignacio. They examined the bodies scattered around the camp. All were dead.

'Well, I guess we broke the gang up at that. I can't see them reforming now that Ignacio is in custody and their pals are dead. Well done, Deputy Postlewaite, you make one slick lawman.'

The pain in Leo's jaw was so bad he did not reply. Phil Morgan rummaged in his bags and come up with a small oilskin package and a flask.

'Put your head to one side while I pour some of this whiskey into that cut.'

'Can't I drink some first?'

Morgan grinned and handed the flask to Leo.

'Drink as much as you like, son. This is gonna hurt you more than it does me.'

Leo almost fainted with the pain as the lawman patiently sewed his cut with silk thread and a needle. His face felt numb but he was not sure if it was the whiskey he had poured into himself or the liquor the sheriff had emptied onto the gash on his jaw. He could feel the tug of the needle as the sheriff worked on him drawing the edges of the cut together with the thread.

'You gonna look one mean son of a bitch with that scar on your phizog. You won't need to pull your gun on lawbreakers. All you'll need to do is leer at them and they'll be so scared they'll ask to be locked up.'

'Thanks,' Leo mumbled, 'you sure cheer up a fella as has just faced death and near enough got himself killed in the process.'

The sheriff laughed and began to pack things away.

'Let's get this critter back to Denton and behind bars. I can't see his friends coming back for more punishment in order to rescue him but I been wrong before.'

They found the bandits' horses about a hundred yards from their camp and tied their captive on to his saddle. Then, with Leo nursing a painful jaw and a throbbing head, they set off for Denton.

# 12

Leo sat on a bench and worked on his weapons. Oil and rags were placed beside him, as were parts of his Colt. The carbine lent to him by the sheriff was propped against the wall awaiting his attention. From time to time he looked towards the activity in the cell which was clearly visible from where he sat.

Their captive sat on the bench-bed glowering while the doctor worked on his head. Also in the cell was Sheriff Phil Morgan with a pistol loosely held in one hand watching the doctor tend the bandit chief.

'Well, his skull's still intact, that's for sure. No signs of concussion as far as I can see. A few days' rest and he'll be fit to go out robbing again,' the doctor remarked.

He left the cell ahead of Morgan and waited patiently while the sheriff locked his prisoner inside.

'I'll send over some headache pills for the prisoner. But you dole them out as he requests them. You don't want him taking an overdose. Now you, young fella.' The doctor turned to Leo. 'Let's take a look at that face of yours.'

Leo obediently sat as the doctor critically examined the wound. The young cowboy's beard was growing out and the knife slash was not so discernible through the thickening hair.

'Mmmm . . . not the neatest of stitching I've ever seen. I'll leave well enough alone. Look in on me in a few days and I'll decide when the stitches come out.'

The doctor picked up his bag.

'The best medicine I can give you is the advice to find yourself another job. The next knife could be a bit lower and then your damned head will come off. Morgan won't be able to sew that back on no matter what he claims.'

'Doc, you already told him that,' interjected Morgan, and grinned at Leo. 'This young'un, he's already saved my life before he took on the job and then this goddamned morning he up and pops away with his Colt and damned well saves my bacon again.'

Leo noticed a movement from the cell and turned to see the prisoner staring at him with malignant eyes.

'You the fella as shot up my men out in the street?'

Leo did not answer, but stared with some curiosity at the man in the cell now gripping the bars of his prison and glaring at him.

The notorious bandit chief had a blunt and rudely tanned handsome face framed by a shock of pale-gold hair. It was a face battered by high winds in mountain passes – a face scarred by blades but a strangely handsome face nonetheless. Right now it was contorted by hate as those pale eyes stared out at the young cowboy.

'That is twice you have thwarted me, cowboy. The next occasion will see you dead at my feet.'

'That's hardly likely, seeing as you have a date with a rope,' Leo replied steadily, quite unfazed by the man's vehemence. 'Maybe I'll ask for the privilege of kicking your feet from under you. That's what the third encounter will be all about, mister.'

A grim smile creased that dark face.

'No jail is strong enough to contain Ignacio. Even now my men are gathering to come in and rescue me, cowboy. That doc gave you good advice to find another job. But my advice is for you to get on your horse and ride back to where you come from. Even then you won't be able to hide from me. I will find you and then I will take you to an anthill and spread you on top of it. I have done this same thing to men who crossed me. In the end they were begging me to kill them.'

For a moment the two men stared at each other. Leo instinctively knew that while this man lived he would not rest easy in his bed at night.

'Hell, Leo, don't waste your time on that worn-out piece of horse dung,' the sheriff intervened.

Leo turned back to his task of cleaning his weapons, more disturbed than he let on by the exchange with the prisoner.

'Leave that there cleaning for a while, Leo, and come and have a game.'

Since returning to Denton Leo noticed the sheriff had taken to calling him by his first name instead of the usual kid or son.

They sat at a battered desk and Morgan pulled out a dog-eared deck and began to shuffle. The sheriff chucked out a pile of matches and divided them equally between them. As they played poker Leo forgot about the man in the cell.

'I noticed you and Doc playing that night in the Silver Penny.'

The sheriff grinned. 'There's a gang of us meet most nights to play. It's a battle of wits we all enjoy. I figure that's what makes Doc so grumpy 'cos I keep winning.'

They played for a while in silence. Leo's pile of matches slowly diminished.

'Where you from, Leo? You never did rightly say.'

Leo hesitated before answering.

'A bit to the west of here. The nearest town was Ladler. I helped run a big outfit there called Pentland. Owned by a fella name of Cyrus Breen.'

'Uh-huh, what made you leave?'

Again Leo hesitated before answering.

'I guess I made a fool of myself over the owner's daughter.'

Before he knew it Leo was pouring out his story to the sheriff. He finished off with the encounter in town with Claude McQueen.

'I guessed Cyrus could make trouble for me with the law for shooting Claude. I only winged him. There was no way I wanted to kill him. So you see, Sheriff, you may be harbouring a wanted man. I wouldn't want to get you into no trouble.'

Sheriff Morgan grinned across the desk at Leo. The more he got to know the youngster the more he liked him.

'Hell, no lawman would come looking for you in that case. It sounds like a case of self-defence. If anyone needs the law after him it's that Claude McQueen.'

They played in silence for a while.

'This girl you were sweet on, she feel the same about you?' Morgan asked suddenly.

'I . . . I guess so.'

'Why don't you write her and tell her where you are at and that you're safe? She's probably worried out of her mind about you just taking off like that.'

Leo stared for a moment at the lawman. It had never occurred to him to write.

'I . . . I'll think about it,' he said at last.

The prisoner in the cell had lain down on the rude bunk provided for his comfort. Though he feigned sleep he had listened carefully to the young cowboy's tale. Names and locations were filed away. When the time come, information like this could be used to his own advantage, or better still to wreak revenge on the young-ster who had thwarted his plan to rob the bank at Denton. Gingerly he fingered the injuries to his head. The cowboy's death would not be an easy one.

# 13

'Claude, why don't you pay more attention to Imogen? She's a lovely young woman and, furthermore, she is the heir to Pentland.'

Claude frowned at his mother.

'I thought the plan was for you to marry Breen and that would put the ranch in our possession.'

'Yes, yes, I know, but I would like to see you settled down and married.'

'Married!'

Claude pondered this new concept and wondered if this would interfere with his frequent trips into town. He was a regular patron of the bawdy houses and gambling dens of Ladler. Slowly he nodded. He had the impression that Imogen avoided him and could not imagine why. In his own opinion he was an affable young ladies; man.

'Right, Mother, I'll start to work my charm on her.'

'If you hurry you'll just catch her. I saw her getting ready for riding out. Offer to accompany her and make her aware of your high regard for her.'

Claude did as his mother suggested and accosted the young woman as she headed for the stables.

'Miss Imogen, I was just coming to see you. I see you are dressed for riding. How fortunate, for I was about to ask you to ride out with me.'

Imogen stared at the brutish young man before her and tried to keep the dislike from her face.

'Thank you, Claude, but I prefer to ride alone.'

She made to pass by, but Claude was not so easily dismissed. He stepped in front of the girl and blocked her progress.

'There's no need to be nervous of me, Miss Imogen. I realise you are not used to sophisticated folk like Mother and myself. Mostly you are mixing with these low cowhands. I believe your father had to dismiss one of them because he became too familiar with you. I can assure you that you won't ever be bored in my company. I am charming, clever, superior and very witty company. Back in Quantock I was constantly trying to discourage the young ladies who were eager to make a match with me. I am a very eligible bachelor. But you needn't worry that I would ever put you off. In fact, that is why I have come out here especially to give you the benefit of my company. I believe you and I would make a very handsome couple.'

Imogen was frowning in disbelief as the young man made this speech.

'I'm afraid there must be some mistake, Claude. Never

in my wildest imaginings could I ever conceive a relationship with you. You and I are as unlike as . . . as . . .' Imogen searched for some comparison. 'As likely to make a pair as a golden eagle and a buzzard.'

Claude chuckled knowingly.

'You will have your little joke, Miss Imogen. There's no need to play hard to get with me. I am well aware of the fatal attraction I have for the female kind. I'm not your usual rough and ready cowhand: I am a gentleman used to the finer things of life, as you no doubt appreciate. Now, let me escort you to the stables and pick a horse for you. Then we can ride out together and let everyone see what a fine couple we are.'

'Claude, I don't want to go riding with you,' Imogen stated emphatically. 'I never want to go riding with you. In fact, I would live my life very happily if I never laid eyes on you ever again. So if you will please excuse me. I shall proceed to the stables on my own.'

Again Claude laughed out loud.

'My, but you are a sparky little thing.'

He offered Imogen his arm.

'Take my arm so everyone can see how fond we are of each other. You will soon find out that I'm a much finer fellow than that ruffian Postlewaite who was pestering you. What a lucky escape that was for you. The fellow is a wrong one. I have every reason to know it, for he tried to murder me. Lucky for him he showed his true colours and ran like the coward he is when I braced him.'

Twin spots of colour began to burn vividly on Imogen's face. She stepped back a pace from her companion and placed her fists on her hips. Balefully she glared at Claude.

'You braced him!' she said, in a dangerously low voice. 'From what I heard of the incident you tried to back-shoot

Leo only he was too fast for you. When he nicked your arm you squealed like a stuck pig to which you have a remarkable resemblance. You . . . you ain't fit to shine his boots. In fact his dirty laundry is of more significance to me than you are. I . . . I can only think that I hate you. Leo Postlewaite is my love. You are mean and pompous and boastful. All the things Leo is not. So please do not bother me again with your attentions. Save them for someone more worthy of you.'

Neatly side-stepping the young man she marched off with a stiff back and head held high. Claude stared after her his mouth open. Suddenly he snapped his jaws shut. His eyes narrowed and he glared after the retreating Imogen.

'Hates me, does she! Well, we'll see about that. That young filly needs to be roped and corralled and broken in. And I'm the one to do it. Who the hell does she think she is talking to me, Claude McQueen, like that? Not fit to polish his boots! She prefers his dirty laundry to me! You need taking down a peg or two and I'm the fellow to do it, Imogen Breen, with or without your consent. And then when I have tamed you I'll go and find that Leo Postlewaite and give him a fine thrashing.'

He shook his fist in the direction of the retreating girl.

'You'll regret talking to me like that, you young fool. You and Leo will both regret crossing me.'

# 14

Leo looked up as the door opened and Sheriff Morgan walked inside followed by a much older man. He was large, wearing stout work jeans supported by a pair of braces. The buttons of his shirt strained to contain the huge gut he seemed proud to usher before him.

The new young deputy had his boots propped up on a chair. He was engrossed in leafing through the various wanted notices when the men entered.

'Leo, this is Tom Holby. Tom, this is Leo Postlewaite my new deputy.'

'Howdy, Leo, we all heard what you done. We're real proud of you for capturing Ignacio.'

Leo nodded. 'Howdy, Tom.'

'Leo, you and me is going on patrol.'

The sheriff walked to the gun case and took a shotgun and handed it to Holby.

'Tom here will guard the jail while we're out.'

He took another shotgun from the cabinet and broke it and loaded it while the new guard did the same.

'Every night I take a stroll over the town with my deputy. It lets any wrongdoers know the law is watching them. That's how Jake, my previous deputy, came on Ignacio and his gang. Now poor Jake's up in Boot Hill, but that's the risk you take with the job.'

They left the gaol and Morgan stopped outside on the boardwalk.

'Usually one of us walks up each side of the street but seeing as this is your first night we'll do it together.'

They began to walk.

'Keep your eyes peeled for any doors lying open, or windows busted, or anything that strikes you as odd. We don't usually meet with any trouble but it reassures the respectable citizens of Denton when they see me on regular patrol.'

Lights were on in some of the buildings as they progressed down the street. From time to time Morgan would try a door to see if it was secure. Leo peered down side-alleys and examined the far side of the street for anything unusual. He had no idea what he was looking for, but he was quite enjoying the stroll with Sheriff Morgan.

The idea of a badge on his vest was growing on him. And though he had been a reluctant recruit to the job of lawman he was beginning to feel it had certain attractions.

As they walked, from time to time someone would call out a greeting. Sheriff Morgan knew each and every one they encountered and always greeted the person by name.

'How's your arm?' Leo asked.

'It's a bit sore but coming on. How's your jaw?'

Leo rubbed his hand along the side of his face feeling the rough stitching.

'About the same. My beard covers it up so I might just keep it.'

'What, the beard or the scar?' the older man quipped. 'Hell, you're a mite young to be growing face hair. It's all right for me. I'm so ugly it keeps people from being frighted when they meet me.'

Leo grinned and felt the stitches on his face pull.

Sheriff Morgan was anything but ugly. He had a fine straight nose with deep-set eyes and a firm mouth. Leo had to admit the beard suited the older man. He felt his own growth and decided he would leave the decision to shave till the wound on his face had healed.

As they approached the Silver Penny the raucous sounds of revelry intermingled with the pleasant tinkling of a piano thumping out a dance tune. Leo's interest quickened. He had always enjoyed the monthly dances back at Pentland. Among the cowhands who were employed by Cyrus Breen were always to be found a few who played a musical instrument. Old Sandy, the stable hand, was the mainstay of the music scene for he played a mean fiddle.

Phil Morgan could see that his young deputy was stirred by the sounds of carousing. He grinned to himself.

'You like to dance?'

'Sure thing, Sheriff. Back at Pentland we had a dance every month. People used to come from all over. It was good times for everyone.'

With that statement came a wave of nostalgia for the happy times he would never be able to go back to.

'Let's look in and make sure everyone is behaving,' the sheriff said, and pushed through the batwing doors.

The saloon was buzzing with noise. A space had been cleared in the centre of the room and men and women were jigging in lively time to the music. In one corner the pianist was bravely pounding on the ivories. The two lawmen stood and watched for a moment. Leo began to tap his foot to the music. Morgan grinned at his young deputy.

'Why don't you grab a gal and give her a whirl around the dance floor?' The sheriff had to shout to make himself heard.

'Ain't I on duty?'

'Hell, you're entitled to a bit of relaxation. Go ahead. I'll grab a drink and then carry on patrolling on my own.'

Morgan headed for the bar and Leo plunged into the crowd. He spotted a tall, statuesque, blonde girl standing on her own. Not believing his luck he pushed across to her. She looked with some surprise at him when he approached and indicated he wanted to dance with her. For a moment she looked disconcerted then seemed to make up her mind about something and smiled with even, white teeth.

'Sure thing, fella.'

They moved into the crowd and began to pace the lively steps of the dance. She was a good dancer and light on her feet. Leo, with the practice he had gained from the dances back at Pentland, was whirling and jigging with the best of the performers on the floor.

Every now and then a man would become so excited by the music and movement he would give vent to his feelings with a yell or yodel. The piano player's fingers were flying across the keyboard as he egged the crowd on to faster and faster efforts. It was a lively tune and men and women fairly leapt and pranced about on the floor.

At the bar Phil Morgan got himself a whiskey and turned to watch the dancers. The fat barman leaned across and tapped Phil on the shoulder.

'I see your new deputy likes to live dangerously,' he said.

Phil craned his neck in an effort to see what his deputy was doing to cause the barman to make such a remark.

'He's dancing with Red Tulliver's girl,' the barkeep continued.

'Oh no,' the sheriff growled. 'He's sure one for getting himself into trouble.'

'You want to tell him, Morgan?'

'Hell no, he's a big boy now. It'll be interesting to see how he handles this.'

# 15

Unaware of the interest he was causing, Leo was quite blissfully dancing with his charming hostess. For the first time since leaving Pentland, Leo forgot his troubles and even the ache in his jaw where the stitches nestled did not seem so bad. Subtly the packed floor seemed less and less crowded as the dancers swept to the side and left the space to the two dancers so absorbed in each other.

As the young lawman saw this he became more and more flamboyant in his movements. His partner threw back her head and laughed as he swung and weaved around the dance floor. And Leo began to think what a fine couple they made and that was why the dancers were ceasing to accompany him.

In the midst of his cavorting a few wistful moments touched his thoughts and he wished it were another girl he was dancing with – a beautiful, dark beauty he had left behind. Then he dismissed the thought and concentrated on enjoying himself.

It came completely out of the blue when the rough hand seized him by the shoulder and spun him around. Almost at the same time a fist hit him in the side of the head. Fortunately it was his unharmed side, but nevertheless the blow came as a brutal shock in the midst of his enjoyment. Leo stumbled off-balance and went down. Immediately a boot crashed into his unprotected ribs.

Countless seasons wrestling with steers had given Leo quick reactions. Even though he was dazed and his head was ringing from the punch, instinctively he grabbed the booted foot and heaved with his not inconsiderable strength. A large body crashed to the floor and he felt the vibration of the impact through the boards. Curling round he was on his feet on an instant and stood over the man he had toppled.

'You goddamned lobo,' he yelled. 'What the hell you do that for?'

The man on the floor was scrambling to his feet. He had a long, mean face crowned by a mop of unruly red hair. He was heavily built with powerful arms and a bull-neck. His face was beginning to match the colour of his hair and growing redder as he stared at the man he had just tangled with.

'You dancing with my girl,' he said thickly. 'Nobody dances with Wilma! You hear that, nobody!'

'What you on about, you stupid gorilla? This is a dance hall. That's what people do: they dance.'

'Not with Wilma, they don't,' came the reply and, at the same time, the gorilla rushed at Leo.

The move took Leo by surprise and he was borne backwards and crashed into a table. There was a scramble of boots behind him as onlookers scuttled out of the way. The table held for a fraction of a moment and then gave way under the weight of two fully grown men.

Leo went down with a jarring impact with the red-haired man on top. He hooked his fist round and connected with the man's jaw. His opponent grunted but seemed intent on crushing Leo with a bear-like grip as he wrapped his thick muscular arms around him.

With his arms still free Leo was able to concentrate on punching hard and brutal jabs into the man's face. He was really angry now and he punched unmercifully – smashing his hard fist into the jawbone. He could feel his chest constricting as the man tried to ignore the blows to his face and was squeezing with ever more desperate effort.

The increasing pressure on his lungs seemed only to fuel Leo's rage. His hard fists were punching the man's face into a bloody ruin. At the same time Leo brought up his knee into the man's groin. With a roar of a wounded animal the red-haired man was forced to let go his bear hug and try to counter the deputy's punches.

But it was Leo who was the animal now. He was oblivious to the man's blows. It was as if all the frustrations of the last few weeks boiled up in him and he was intent in punishing the man rash enough to attack him. It could only end in one way.

Red tried to break away and get to his feet. As soon as he was free of the man's grip Leo sprung to his feet. Even as his opponent was scrambling up Leo was on him. He let loose a solid punch to the midriff and as the man bent over another hard uppercut to the nose followed up by a sudden right to the jaw brought the big man crashing to the floor.

Leo stood over the beaten bully waiting for him to get up and start again.

'Get up. You ain't had enough yet. I'm gonna whip some manners into you,' he grated out.

His breath was coming in short wheezes but he was ready for more. The blow to the back of his head was completely unexpected. He staggered forward but stayed upright and whirled with his arms windmilling to catch the cowardly attacker. Before he realized who his assailant was his fist caught the girl on the neck as she was poised to bring the bottle down on his head again. With a scream she stumbled sideways and went down, the bottle flying from her hand. Her eyes glowed with loathing.

'Keep your filthy fists away from Red. You're nothing but a bully hiding behind your badge. If I were a man I'd beat you to a pulp.'

Leo stared in amazement at the hellcat glaring hatred at him. It was the girl he had been dancing with but a few moments before the big man had attacked him.

'Goddamn it, he attacked me. I was only defending myself.'

'You're a bully and a coward,' the girl screamed.

A hand touched Leo on the shoulder. He whirled to defend himself against this new attack.

'Whoa there, Leo!'

Sheriff Morgan put up his hands in mock self-defence.

'I suggest you quit while you are ahead. I never knew the man yet could get the better of a female in an argument.'

He took Leo's arm.

'Come on, there's a whole town out there for us to patrol. You'll likely find some more females to fight over.'

Leo cast a baleful glance over his shoulder at the couple and saw the girl cradling the man's head in her arms. Red Tulliver snarled and pushed her away. Leo felt Sheriff Morgan pulling at his arm and allowed himself to be led away.

As he accompanied his boss out on to the street he reflected that life was certainly not dull in the town of Denton. Shootouts with outlaws followed by a sortie after the miscreants and now a fight with a jealous boyfriend.

'Hell, Phil, I never been so battered in my life since becoming a lawman. Does it get any easier?'

Phil Morgan laughed.

'You'll do to ride the trail with, cowboy. I never realized what a wildcat you where when I recruited you.'

'Why didn't you warn me about that gorilla back at the saloon?'

'I tried to, but you seemed to be having such a good time on that dance floor I couldn't catch your eye.'

Phil Morgan clapped Leo on the shoulder and laughed delightedly.

'You're one goddamn hellcat, Leo.'

The two men continued on their tour of the town and Leo could not help reflecting that, in his own robust way, the sheriff was somehow proud of his new deputy.

# 16

'Hey, Ignacio, there's a wanted poster on you here,' Leo suddenly called out. 'Wanted dead or alive.'

There was no response from the bandit. He lay on his bunk with his hands clasped behind his head and his eyes closed.

Left in charge of the office, Leo was leafing through the wanted posters. The thick sheaf of papers fascinated him. He could never get over the fact that so many villains were loose in the community. The range of crimes was vast and varied, from embezzlement to bigamy, thievery and murder.

After calling out to his prisoner and getting no response he went back to studying the posters. His attention was drawn to one in particular. He put it on top of the pile and studied it intently. While he was so engrossed the street door opened and his boss entered.

'Good news, young fella, they're sending a marshal

down from Houston to collect Ignacio.'

Sheriff Morgan walked over to the cell door.

'You hear that, Ignacio? We gonna get shot of you. The Houston boys want the privilege of hanging you. Pity, I'd have liked to see you swing for Jake, the man you shot out in the street there.'

Ignacio slowly sat up and swung his legs off the bunk. His crudely handsome face bore a mocking grin.

'Sheriff, I shot your deputy like I would a dog an' I'll do the same with his replacement. I'm just biding my time here. My day will come. Might even take over the job of sheriff myself.'

Sheriff Morgan glared back at the prisoner.

'Goddamn fella's overdue a hanging. That rope will shut your no-good mouth for good. Why don't you do one good thing before you depart this earth and tell us who your contact in town is? That's one varmint I sure would like to get behind these bars.'

Turning from the cell the sheriff came over and stood by the desk. Leo obediently rose to allow his boss to sit at the desk.

'What you mean about his contact in town?' Leo asked, as the sheriff sat down.

'Ah, someone from town was feeding him information about movements of money and gold. He always knew where to strike. I've suspected all sorts of people but can't finger nobody. That person's as much guilty of all the crimes as Ignacio. I would sleep easier in bed of a night if I knew who the sneaking polecat is.'

Leo glanced across at the prisoner scowling at them from his cell.

'He'll never tell. He's too mean to do anyone a good turn.'

He turned back and pointed to the sheaf of papers.

'That poster there on top, Phil, I been studying it. I can't say for certain but I reckon I know that one.'

Phil Morgan sat and picked up the poster.

'Bernice Quartermain wanted for embezzlement, four counts of bigamy and suspected murder.'

The lawman read the description and the details of the reward before looking up at his young deputy.

'Go on.'

'A month or so before I left Pentland, Cyrus Breen brought home a woman who sounds a lot like the woman they're describing in that there poster. Calls herself Victoria McQueen.'

Leo bent over and tapped the poster.

'It says here she goes under various aliases.'

He rested his hands on the desk and gazed thoughtfully at the photo.

'Now I think on it, everything between Imogen and me began to go astray shortly after her arrival. She seemed to be everywhere we were. I thought nothing of it at the time but now I wonder was she spying on Imogen and myself and then reporting back to Cyrus.'

Sheriff Morgan stroked his beard as he regarded his young deputy.

'Hell, Leo, the way you describe this fella Breen he's a mighty rich man – a juicy target for an unscrupulous female. What you think?'

Leo straightened up and stared with troubled eyes at the sheriff. Suddenly his eyes widened.

'She sent for her son. It was him as I had the fight with. Damnation, you think she wants to hitch her son up with Imogen? Claude marries Imogen and Victoria marries Cyrus. If I'm right and that happens I figure she'll either clean Breen out, or have him bumped off and then every-thing belongs to them.'

Sheriff Morgan leaned back in his chair.

'You sure you're not making all this up, Leo? Could be you're mistaken about this Victoria McQueen.' His eyes widened. 'Victoria McQueen – Queen Victoria, that's the British Queen. She's been in the papers in recent months, can't recollect exactly what for. If you were hunting round for a name that might just come to mind. Hell, Leo, let's send a wire to Houston. Ask them for the latest low-down on this bird. If she is this Bernice Quartermain, it sounds as if your friends could be courting trouble. Get over to the telegraph office. Sam will know who to send it to. I'll look after things here.'

There was a letter for Leo when he got to the general store after sending the wire. He felt a fluttering of his insides as he saw the writing. He knew it was his old friend Broderick. He had sent a letter to Imogen via his sidekick for fear of Cyrus intercepting it. Now he had the reply he feared to open it. Not wanting anyone to see him he wandered down to the livery stable and sat on the water butt left outside for thirsty travellers.

For a long time he sat staring at the envelope afraid to open it. He was half tempted to walk up to the Silver Penny and have a drink but there would be no privacy there. At last he took out his knife and slit the envelope.

A large piece of paper covered with a bold masculine hand was revealed. Hiding his disappointment he unfolded the sheet.

Unnoticed, a smaller, folded sheet fluttered to the ground to settle between his booted feet. Leo read the letter.

*Dear Leo*

*It sure was good to hear from you. When you coming back to Pentland? We shore miss you. I give your letter to Miss Imogen. She was teary eyed about it. I believe she misses you as much as me. Claude McQueen has your old job. I think Mr Breen has lost his senses. He leaves the running of things to Claude. Claude couldn't run a herd of sheep. He knows as much of cattle ranching as my horse knows about Shakespeare. While Claude makes a sheep's backside of the ranch Cyrus is off riding and shopping with Mrs McQueen. He's shore besotted with that female. Mind she's a fine-looking filly. She could besot me all she liked.*

*Come back soon.*

*Your old sidekick Broderick.*


For long a long time Leo sat on the barrel staring into the distance. It was with some effort he stood up and walked back down to the jailhouse. There was a bad feeling inside him. In spite of all that had happened back at Pentland he was fearful for the friends he had left behind there.

'Goddamn it, if that Victoria or Bernice is behind all my troubles. . . .'

The bad feeling stayed with him.

Back at the livery the stable hand came out to breathe in the fresh air of the evening. A piece of paper fluttered into his notice. Making sure he wasn't overlooked he picked it up and went back into the stables. Inside he carefully examined his find. He held the paper up to the light and read the letter that had been meant for Leo.

Gone was the vacant look of the idiot. In its place was the sly expression of a man who knows quite well what he is about. Thoughtfully he placed the paper inside his jacket.

# 17

Leo looked up as the street door opened. Two men in tall hats and wearing riding boots with jingling spurs entered. Leo leant back in the chair and let his hand drop casually on to his thigh so it rested near his holstered revolver. There was something about the men that bred such reaction. They gave out an air of hard-bitten competence and restrained power. Then there was their size that made one instinctively back off. They seemed to fill the office with their presence. Planed features with hard cold eyes stared down at the young deputy.

'You in charge here?'

'Yeah.' Leo tried to sound nonchalant. 'What can I do for you gents?'

The man leaned down towards Leo.

'It ain't what you can so for us, fella, it's what we can do for you.'

The cold eyes stared at Leo for a moment or two as if daring the youngster to say more.

Leo stared the man out, not wanting to seem intimidated. At last the man straightened up as if satisfied he had done enough to put Leo in his place. He swept back his coat to reveal a badge pinned to his waistcoat.

'US Marshal Tom Grover, and my sidekick here is Marshal Aidan Perry. You got a prisoner we taking back to Houston.'

Leo got up from his chair, grateful to have the men identified as law officers and not potential troublemakers.

'Glad to meet you, Marshal. My name's Leo Postlewaite,

deputy to Sheriff Morgan.'

Leo offered his hand. Grover either did not see it or chose to ignore Leo's gesture of friendship.

'Where is this piece of filth we got to transport?'

'Right there.' Leo pointed to the cell.

Ignacio, as usual, was lying indolently on his bunk. He took no notice of the men who had entered the building.

'Open up,' the marshal ordered Leo.

The youngster hesitated.

'You got papers or something authorizing you?'

The hard eyes were turned fully on Leo. A finger of one hand pointed to his badge while the other hand slipped on to the butt of the Peacemaker strapped to his side.

'These are my authorization, sonny boy. Now, do what you're told while you're still able to move without the aid of crutches.'

Leo's eyes narrowed and instinctively he stepped back so that both lawmen were spaced each side of him.

'Mister, I ain't been a lawman long, but one thing I learned in that time is, in this office I say what goes. Now if you want to take custody of that there prisoner you show me some proper papers and then if I think they're in order, then, and only then, you may interview the prisoner.'

Marshal Grover's lips shaped into a sneer.

'You wet-assed puppy, I've been a lawman since afore your mammy was wiping your backside. Nobody talks to a United States marshal like that. You need respect, boy. I'm gonna pistol-whip you for sassing me like that.'

Nobody noticed the prisoner had risen from his reclining position and was watching with some interest the confrontation taking place in the office. There was slight smile on his face and he licked his lips as if in anticipation.

74

Leo had stepped back and was trying to keep an eye on both of the marshals. He was not sure why the big lawman was being so aggressive but was determined not to be cowed by the two men who had pushed so abruptly into the normally peaceful sheriff's office.

Grover was coming round the desk, his face tight with anger. Instinctively Leo grabbed the chair and swung it with all his force at the lawman. Expecting Leo to fold before his aggressive behaviour the move took the marshal by surprise.

Leo was no lightweight pushover. He was almost as big as the marshal. The heavy wooden chair smashed into the lawman's arm and twisted him partway round. Leo reached forward, grabbed the man's lapel and yanked him forward on to the top of the desk. He let go the chair and slammed his freed fist into the marshal's face. Grover yelled in hurt surprise but was helpless to defend himself as Leo hit him twice more.

He saw the second man moving towards him and kicked the fallen chair into the path of the advancing lawman. Perry put out a hand to knock the chair out of his way and at the same time pulled his Peacemaker. Leo froze. With one hand holding Glover and the other bunched into a fist ready to strike the marshal again there was no way he could pull his own weapon. He stayed where he was watching Perry's eyes.

'Let him go,' the big man gritted out.

Slowly, Leo reversed till his back was against the wall. Marshal Grover slowly rose from the desk. His eyes were glittering with malicious intent as he massaged his damaged arm while at the same time working his jaw where Leo's fist had smacked him.

'Sonny Jim, you've just booked yourself into a hospital

bed. I'm gonna beat you to within an inch of your life. It'll be months before you throw a punch on anyone again. Keep that pistol on him, Aidan, while I teach him a lesson he won't forget in a hurry.'

Leo could only watch helplessly while the marshal moved round the desk towards him. He tensed himself ready to fight his corner. The advancing marshal pulled his Peacemaker.

'I guess I'll have to alter your face somewhat for you. You seem far too pretty to be a lawman.'

'Hold it right there!'

The voice came from the doorway. All the men in the office turned towards the speaker.

Sheriff Morgan stood in the doorway, a Colt held in one hand. Cautiously he stepped further inside the room, carefully keeping his gun trained on the two strangers. Slowly he nodded his head as he recognized the men he was confronting.

'Grover and Perry, well, well, well, just put up those irons. This is my jail and I'll have no gunplay in here.'

'Morgan, I might have guessed we'd find you sheriff in a one-horse town. Can't you do any better than this?'

Morgan walked inside. He kept his Colt on the two lawmen until they took the hint and put away their weapons.

'What's going on here?'

'Hell, I was just teaching this young puppy some manners. You robbing the orphanage now, Morgan, to get your deputies? I guess no right thinking, grown man would work with you.'

Morgan looked shrewdly at the red weals on the lawman's face and the trickle of blood seeping down into the bush of his moustache.

'Lucky I came in when I did before my deputy did any more damage to you two lugheads. Don't you know who this is? This is Post Mortem Postlewaite. He don't take in anyone alive. Hell, he ain't twenty yet and he's already killed nine men.'

He turned to Leo.

'Damn it, Leo, you don't try and kill lawmen, do you hear! They're on our side. Just keep killing the outlaws. Leave the lawmen to get on with the business of keeping the peace.'

Leo said nothing; just stared angrily at the two lawmen. The sheriff turned his attention back to the two marshals.

'I take it you two have come to take our star prisoner back to Houston. You got the proper warrants?'

With ill-grace Grover fished out the papers he had been so reluctant to show Leo. Morgan nodded as he glanced over them.

'Everything seems in order.'

He pointed to the cells. 'There's your man.'

The marshals walked across to look in at Ignacio.

'So this is the murdering sumbitch we gotta take back for hanging. Sure don' look like much. Can't see why it took so long for you to catch him, Morgan. Mebbe you just getting too old and slow.'

'Guess you could be right at that. It took Post Mortem here to bag him. It's lucky you got him to take back. I had to stop Post Mortem from stiffing him otherwise you'd be hauling a corpse back to Houston. It takes me all my time restraining him from killing. I sure hope he stays on this side of the law. I sure as hell wouldn't like to be the one to have to bring him in if'n he goes bad.'

There was a growing wariness in the eyes of the men from Houston as they looked at Morgan's deputy.

Leo kept his face mean and glared at the men, feigning hatred, which wasn't hard to do after his abortive run in with the lawmen. Morgan unlocked the cell.

'He's all yours, men. Just get him safely back to Houston.'

Grover dragged Ignacio out of the cell and held him while his partner put a set of cuffs on him. With his prisoner safely cuffed the lawman punched the bandit hard in the stomach. Ignacio grunted and went over as Grover's knee came up to hit him in the face.

'You piece of slime, you make a false move at anytime and I'll beat you to death.'

Ignacio leaned against the bars of the cell and groaned. Grover grabbed his shoulders and thrust him roughly towards the front of the office.

'Be seeing you, Sheriff. Maybe we'll meet up with your deputy sometime and teach him not to mess with us again.'

By this time they were exiting the office.

'Make sure it's in daylight, Grover, and you got a posse to back you up,' Sheriff Morgan called, as the door slammed behind the lawmen. He turned and grinned at Leo. 'Now, Post Mortem, tell me what the hell was going on in here when I arrived. Seems to me you invite trouble like horse droppings attract flies.'

# 18

The stable hand looked up in some surprise as he saw the lawmen drag Ignacio off the street and slam him against a wall. They took it in turns to punch the handcuffed man. Ignacio sagged and would have fallen only one of the men would support him while the other punched. Finally they stepped back and Ignacio crumpled into the straw, his face a mess of bruises.

'We hate all greasers and especially murdering greasers. So every day we'll have us a little punching session with you just to remind you to behave while in our custody. What we would most like is for you to make a break for it. Then we could shoot you like the dog you are and that would save everyone a lot of bother.'

Marshal Grover turned to the stable boy.

'We need those horses we ordered. You got them ready?'

The young man nodded with owlish eyes fixed on the bloody figure on the floor. He led the men outside and pointed to three mounts tethered to the hitching rail.

'Help him on his horse.'

Glover and his partner mounted and waited for the stable boy to comply with his order. The youngster knelt beside the beaten outlaw.

As he helped the bandit to his feet he slipped a piece of paper inside the bandit's pocket. Ignacio leaned heavily on the youth as he assisted him to his horse. It was with some difficulty he accomplished the task of mounting. The youth spent some time placing Ignacio's feet in the stirrups. The lawmen were unsighted as he slid the long stiletto inside the bandit's boot.

Finally the trio were ready and they rode up the main street on the first leg of the journey that looked like being a long and painful ride for Ignacio.

It was a three-day ride to Houston from Denton. Grover and Perry were in no hurry. They had bought supplies to sustain them on their stopovers.

Once out of Denton and out of sight of any observation they looped a rope around the neck of their prisoner and fastened the end to the harness of Perry's horse.

'Seems a mite subdued. You think he's sulking, Tom?'

'Maybe we should drag him for a piece,' Grover answered, giving the rope a vicious tug.

'Please, *señor*, I not give you trouble. I will be the model prisoner,' Ignacio pleaded through swollen lips.

'You goddamn right you'll be the model prisoner, or you'll be a dead prisoner,' Grover growled, giving the rope another yank. 'And who gave you permission to speak? Did I say you could talk?'

Each sentence was accompanied by a hard jerk on the rope. The prisoner had to grip the saddle with his manacled hands to stay on his horse.

When they stopped that night Ignacio was tossed to the ground and left. He lay exhausted and watched the lawmen set up camp. From time to time he groaned as if the discomfort of his bruises was too much for him. He was offered no food or drink and asked for none, fearing to bring upon himself the rough attention of the lawmen. Before they settled into their blankets they secured the prisoner to a tree by the rope around his neck.

'We're real heavy sleepers, Mex, so you can make a break for it in the night.'

'*Si, señor.*'

Ignacio curled up at the base of the tree and slept soundly. He was rudely kicked awake at first light.

'Still here, Mex? Goddamn thought we might lose you last night we slept so heavy.'

'Thank you, *señor*, I need to go in the bush. My bladder it is bursting.'

This request brought him another kick.

'Hell, piss your britches then.'

'Please, *señor*, I no like that; I am a clean man.'

'Huh, a clean Mex, that'll be a change.'

'Hell, let him go, Aidan. I don't care to drag a piss-stink prisoner all the way to Houston.'

Grumbling loudly, Marshal Perry untied the rope and holding one end walked into the bushes with his prisoner.

'That's far enough.'

'*Si, señor.*'

Ignacio looked around uncertainly.

'I need private please.'

Perry drew his Peacemaker.

'Goddamn you, Mex, I oughta shoot you now and save any more bother.'

Ignacio cowered away from the pistol, a look of abject terror on his face.

'Please don't shoot, Marshal. I need go bad but I need private.'

'Goddamn you, Mex, you're sure more bother than you're worth.'

Perry cocked the pistol. He pointed at some under-growth.

'OK, go in there but I'm keeping a tight hold on this rope. You hurry up. At the slightest hint of trouble I'll fill you full of lead.'

'*Si, señor*, I hurry. Thank you, thank you.'

Nodding obsequiously Ignacio scurried in behind the foliage.

'Thank you, *señor*.' His voice was muffled coming out from behind the shrubs.

With a look of disgust on his face Marshal Perry aimed the Peacemaker at the point where the prisoner's voice was coming from. For a moment he was tempted to fire into the bush just for the hell of it but managed to restrain himself and instead sent a steady stream of abuse towards the prisoner. The rope quivered and grew taut in his grip as the prisoner squatted to relieve himself. A groan of relief came from behind the bush.

'Jesus,' Marshal Perry blasphemed, and stared out into the trees.

There was a slight movement beside him and he turned. He blinked in surprise. The man who should have been on the end of the rope was beside him and pushing a slim blade against his throat.

'This blade is long and sharp, Marshal.'

Ignacio pushed and the blade went in a half inch. Perry went very still.

'When I drive it up beneath your chin it should be long enough to reach your brain. Depending on what part of the brain the blade enters you will either die instantly or you will become paralysed. I have experiment with this method many times. No two times are the same. Now you will just let the hammer on that Colt down very gently. Then you will hand it to me even more carefully. After that we will join your friend for breakfast.'

Gone was the subservient peon and the Mexican accent. In its place was a voice resolute with intent. Marshal Perry did as he was told. Ignacio nodded in satisfaction.

'You walk round behind there where I went.'

With Perry in front they went to the bush. Ignacio sliced the rope where he had tied it to a branch and looped the end loosely around his neck.

'Now we go to breakfast. You will hold this rope as if everything was as it was before.'

'Hell, Perry, what the hell's keeping you? Breakfast's about ready,' Grover yelled from the camp.

Ignacio smiled at his captive.

'Tell him you are coming now.'

'I'm on my way, Tom.'

They emerged from the trees and to the casual glance of Marshal Grover everything was as it should be. Perry still held the rope and the prisoner stumbled dejectedly behind him. He turned his attention back to the fire and the sizzling pan of bacon.

Ignacio raised the Peacemaker and slashed it across the back of Perry's head. The marshal stumbled and fell. Grover looked up in surprise and was staring into the levelled barrel of his partner's pistol. His hand darted to his own gun and Ignacio casually shot him in the knee.

Marshal Grover screamed and sat back abruptly, both hands clasped around his leg. Blood stained his fingers as he stared white-faced at the Mexican bandit with the smoking pistol in his hand.

'That bacon sure smells good. Thank you, Marshal. Now if you would just find me the key to these handcuffs I will be able to eat my breakfast in comfort.'

'Go to hell, greaser!'

Again Ignacio fired. Again the marshal screamed as the heavy bullet smashed the other leg. He rolled around in agony.

'Oh my God, oh my God. Don't shoot any more. I'll get you the goddamn key.'

'Careful now, just set the key on the ground and I'll retrieve it, Marshal. Don't you make any sudden movements or I'll be obliged to shoot your elbows out.'

Freed of his cuffs, Ignacio frisked the wounded lawman and removed his weapons.

'Help me stop the bleeding. I don't wanna bleed to death.'

'All things in their place, Marshal. First I have to secure your friend here.'

The bandit pulled the dazed Perry's arms behind his back and fastened his wrists with the handcuffs. He stood and kicked the man and he groaned and tried to roll over. Ignacio kicked him again and moved to the fire. He helped himself to the bacon and coffee.

'You gotta help me stop this bleeding. It ain't stopping on its own.'

'All in good time, my friend. I have not had any food or drink in two days. I am so hungry I reckon I'll eat all the bacon and I'm so thirsty I'll probably drink the whole pot of coffee.'

With a sigh of contentment Ignacio stretched out beside the fire.

'I was so cold last night tied to that tree I hardly slept a wink.'

'You gotta get me to a doctor. I'll bleed to death if I don't get help soon.'

'Jesus, Tom, are you hurt?'

Marshal Perry had regained his senses.

'The goddamn greaser shot me in the legs. I'm bleeding to death.'

'Why don't you help him, you Mex bastard?'

'He is in a bad way, amigo. I shot him in the knees. He may never walk again. Perhaps he will lose his job as a marshal. Then he would not be able to kick helpless prisoners. You know, I ache all over from that beating – my stomach, my balls, my ribs, my head, my face. This salty bacon is stinging my poor, split lips like hell. Perhaps I shall take a little rest before deciding what to do with you.'

'If you ride away now, Mex, we promise we won't come after you. We'll just ride on into Houston and tell them you managed to escape.'

Ignacio took a paper from his pocket. He held it up to his nose and smelt it. A smile lit his battered face. He unfolded the letter that Imogen had written to Leo. There was a faraway look in his eyes when he finished reading. He sat staring off into the distance ignoring the pleading from his prisoners.

# 19

'Ignacio, it's Ignacio, he's back.'

The bandit leader had ridden into his stronghold with three good horses all saddled and bridled. He also brought with him two Peacemakers, two carbines and two Bowie knives.

His gang gathered round excitedly slapping their leader on the back and plying him with questions.

'Hold on, amigos, I am very thirsty. I think it must be many days since I have a drink of tequila.'

Gathered round their leader like children reunited with a fond parent the bandits crowded inside the cantina.

'You look as if you had a hard time, Ignacio. Your face bears the marks of a beating. Did the gringos do that?'

'*Si*, they are very cruel those Americanos. They beat poor helpless Mexican prisoners. I tell you now, amigos, do not let the gringo lawmen take you prisoner. It is better to die from a bullet than rot in a gringo jail.'

'How did you escape, Ignacio? Did you have to kill many gringos to get away?'

Ignacio took a long swig of fiery liquor before answering. He walked to a table and hooking a chair sat and faced his men.

'For many days I lay in the stinking jail. Each day I knew my fearless band of men would ride into Denton and rescue me. Each day I grew more and more confident that you were plotting a great rescue. You would dynamite the jail and I would walk free over the bodies of the lawman Morgan and his deputy Leo Postlewaite.

'After a week went by I knew then you were gathering a great force of gunmen to lay siege to the jail. You would overwhelm the sheriff and unlock my prison. I dreamed of taking that Morgan and Postlewaite and hanging them for their crimes. But, amigos, the days went by and my men never rode to the gringo jail to free me. I was forced to the conclusion that there would be no rescue coming for me.'

The bandit chiefs rudely handsome face had a deceptively mild frown as he stared at his followers. The unsavoury band of desperados hung with weapons and drooping moustaches stared back at him. Before his steady and scornful gaze, they glanced at each other furtively and then shifted their feet uneasily. No one answered his unspoken challenge. Ignacio took another drink before continuing.

'So, unable to rely on my comrades in arms, what does a resourceful man do? I tell you what I do. I had to rig my own rescue.'

Before Ignacio could further harangue his men there was a disturbance from outside. A shadow darkened the doorway and all heads swivelled towards the figure standing just inside.

He was big, with a round brutal face that had not seen a razor for days. The eyes were small and bloodshot. Beneath his sombrero could be seen large protruding ears. Right now his mouth was down-turned in an ugly grimace as he stared with undisguised dislike at the returned bandit chief.

'Morales,' Ignacio called out,' you are just in time to drink to my return. I was just calling my men's loyalty into question and wondering why no one came to my rescue when I was in the gringo jail.'

The big man took another step inside. He was a veritable giant and towered over all the men inside the cantina.

'Ignacio,' he finally growled, 'no one went after you as nobody wanted you back. You're no longer leader here. While you were away I took over as leader of the gang.'

Ignacio tipped back his chair and contemplated the giant.

'Is that a fact?'

He turned his gaze to the men at the bar.

'You men agreed to this hulk taking my place as leader?'

'We did not know what to think, Ignacio. Jorge and Thornaso came back from Denton and told of a gun battle with some of our comrades killed. They told us of a famous gunfighter joined up with Sheriff Morgan and shot your band to pieces. Then there was another fight when the posse from Denton caught up and killed more of our comrades. We thought you were dead.'

'You lie, Pedro. Our brother Jason would have passed word back to you of my fate.'

In the uneasy silence that followed this bald accusation Morales shuffled forward. His eyes were bloodshot and it was obvious he had been drinking heavily.

'Get out, Ignacio. You are finished here. I am leader now.'

The giant stood swaying unsteadily before the deposed leader. Ignacio nodded emphatically then stood upright.

'I see. Perhaps I could say goodbye to Lamar?'

For the first time the giant smiled. It was a cruel and malicious smile.

'Sure thing, Ignacio.' He turned his head and yelled in a stentorian voice. 'Lamar!'

For a few moments nothing happened and then a slight female figure entered the cantina. She stood with bowed head just inside the doorway.

'Lamar, it is me, your old lover Ignacio. Have you no word of greeting for me?'

Her long, luxurious hair hung down over her face obscuring her features. Morales swung round and grabbed her by the arm and tugged her forward. With a quick gesture he gripped her hair and jerked it back with a vicious tug. There was silence in the room as everyone stared at the young girl. Her eyes were blackened and almost closed from the puffiness around them. Blood had caked on the side of her face and on her split and swollen lips.

'It looks to me as if you had a slight accident, Lamar. Was it a wall you walked into?' Ignacio asked softly.

Morales laughed then – a harsh and brutal snorting.

'My fist, amigo, she ran into my fist. Several times she kept putting her face in the way of my fist. It was a long time before I could make her stop doing it but in the end we came to an arrangement. She agreed to do what I wanted and then my fist stopped hitting her face.'

Ignacio set his glass upon the table.

'When I took over as leader I had to challenge the man

who was in charge. Emile was his name. We fought a duel. Fortunately for me I won and so became leader.'

Ignacio smiled a cold cruel smile.

'It seems to me, Morales, you should extend the same courtesy to me and give me a chance to defend my title.'

Morales stared at Ignacio with a frown on his brutal face.

'What are you saying, little man?'

'I'm saying, Morales, that you should have challenged me to a duel to win the leadership of my gang. It does not seem right that you should just take it without some effort to show you are the right man for the job.'

Morales snorted. 'You mean you want me to kill you, little man.'

The new leader was growing in confidence. Ignacio was no longer a feared leader but just a little man to be put down.

'A good leader must be afraid of no one. He must prove he is a fearless fighter. It is very simple. We will fight – you and me. The man who wins will become leader of the gang.'

A slow smile spread over Morales' face. 'You want me to kill you, is that what you are saying?'

Ignacio shook his head.

'No, no, you ox, we will fight and you will die and I shall resume leadership of Ignacio's feared band of despera-dos.'

He turned and walked outside. The men in the cantina had no option but to follow him.

# 20

The sun beat down hot and strong out of a cloudless sky. Already the men from the cantina were sweating in the fierce heat. They lined each side of the street. An air of excitement that enlivens all mobs when violent confrontation is impending was discernible. There was an agitated shuffling as men jockeyed for a better position to view the fight.

Ignacio stood with cool aplomb. Carefully he removed his hat and then his jacket and handed them to one of the bystanders. Morales, already in his shirtsleeves, glared with undisguised hatred at his opponent.

'How do you want to die, little man?'

Ignacio pursed his lips thoughtfully.

'I think I would like to die peacefully in my bed with a beautiful girl by my side. I will make love to her for the last time. Then I will drink a bottle of tequila and call for the priest to come and give me absolution for the sins of my past life. After that I will close my eyes and with my rosary clasped in my hands I will go to meet my God with a soul pure as driven snow.' He sighed. 'Ah, that would be a beautiful death.'

Morales frowned. 'You are mad, little man. You are going to die today in this street with me kicking out your life like I would a dog.'

'How do you want to fight, Morales? Do you want knives, guns, or bare hands?'

The giant straightened from the fighting crouch he had adapted since stepping into the street. He frowned and blinked as if it had never occurred to him how he was to fight the disgraced leader.

'It is the privilege of the challenger to choose the weapons,' Ignacio explained, seeing the puzzlement on the big man's face. 'It is very simple. You are challenging me. You want to take over my gang. How do you want me to kill you? Do you prefer a bullet in the head, a knife in the gut, or an old-fashioned thrashing with bare fists?'

Morales looked down at his big hands with fingers as long as the tines on a hayfork. Slowly he curled them into huge fists. It looked like he could hammer fence posts into the ground without the aid of a sledge. He looked up at Ignacio with a sudden light in his eyes.

'I will kill you with my bare fists, little man.'

Ignacio spread his arms wide.

'Let us disarm then.'

He unbuckled the gunbelt that had once adorned the waist of a United States marshal and handed it to a bystander. Morales did the same with his weapon. He stood legs astride with arms curled, looking confidently at the man he was about to mangle.

Ignacio danced about a little, punching into the air as if he were warming up. Suddenly he stepped forward and swiftly kicked the big Mexican hard between his spread-out legs. Morales gasped and grabbed his injured parts, bending over in agony. The same boot that had crushed his gonads smashed into his face crushing his nose.

Morales roared in anger and pain, thrashing his arms wildly to catch his opponent. But Ignacio was no longer in front of him. The bandit chief had ducked behind Morales and with the same tremendous force again kicked Morales between the legs only this time from behind.

The big man bent over again, his breath wheezing as he

tried to contain the pain. That ready boot planted itself squarely in the seat of his pants. It was too much for the big bruiser. He went down on his hands and knees, whining in agony as he tried to ease the pain in his injured groin.

His tormentor danced around him and kicked him in the side of the head. The big man came off his hands and onto his knees. As he roared out his pain and tried to regain his feet, Ignacio stepped up behind him and clapped his cupped hands hard on to the big man's ears. Then he stepped back and kicked again, this time hitting Morales in the base of the neck. The bruiser's head jerked violently with the force of the kick and he pitched forward into the dust. He was moaning in frustration, pain and anger as he tried to push himself up. Blood and sweat dripped from his face into the dust of the street. He shook his head and groaned aloud.

Ignacio stepped back and contemplated the big man.

'Have you had enough, Morales?'

'I'll kill you! Why don't you fight fair? Stand and fight like a man.'

Ignacio laughed.

'Is that what you said to Lamar, Morales? Did you ask her to fight like a man as you beat her? You are a bully and a coward. I will not kill you. I will be generous and let you live. When men see you they will point to you and say, there is the woman fighter. He is brave when he is beating women, but when a man faces up to him he bleeds into the dust. Everywhere you go men will scorn you. So go. Leave here at once. I never want to see your face around here again, or I will kill you as I would a dog as you threatened to do to me.'

Morales was weeping in pain and frustration at his defeat.

'I will kill you . . .' he ground out. 'I will kill you, Ignacio, for this.'

Ignacio turned from the beaten man and began to recover his possessions. A slim figure darted past him. The bandit chief whirled back to the street again.

A young woman hurled herself on to the bent back of Morales. With one hand she gripped him by the hair. In the other hand was a long steel blade. Morales was taken by surprise as was everyone in the street. The girl tugged at the big man's hair. Weakened by the beating he had taken, Morales was slow to react. He reached behind him for the woman clinging to his back. His neck was arched and exposed. It was obvious to everyone but Morales what the girl intended. They watched in hypnotic helplessness as she drew the blade hard across the exposed neck.

The skin parted like an opening mouth. She had struck hard and true. The jugular was severed. A jet of blood spurted out from the gaping wound and played onto the dust of the street. Morales opened his mouth to scream or call out but only succeeded in producing a gurgling noise as blood welled into his mouth from the dreadful wound in his neck. The head came back further and further as the girl kept her hold on the hair and sawed frantically with her deadly blade.

No one moved as they watched Morales struggling feebly to dislodge the slight figure of the girl clinging to his back. She seemed intent on severing the big man's head from his shoulders. Deeper and deeper the blade hewed.

No man, no matter how strong, could withstand such injuries. Morales swayed sideways, his hands pawing the air and his mouth open in a silent scream. He pitched onto his face. His body jerked and twitched in the dust. Slowly the girl released her grip and stepped back still holding the knife. Blood dripped from the blade as she held it by her side and watched the death throes.

'Pig,' she spat out, 'you will beat no more women.'

A great sigh went up from the onlookers. The girl turned and looked at Ignacio. He was regarding her quizzically with a faint smile on his face.

'I was your woman and he wanted me to become his woman. When I resisted he did this.'

She pointed to her battered face.

'I know you hate me, Ignacio,' she said, a great sadness evident in her voice.

'Why would I hate my beautiful little pigeon? If when I returned and you had no bruises then I might have been angry.'

He reached out a hand to her.

'Come, we will drink to this great victory.'

She moved hesitantly to his side. He put his arm around her and turned towards the entrance of the cantina.

'Come, my loyal followers,' he called. 'I have learnt of a very rich ranchero with many cattle and much riches and a foolish old man who owns it. It is ripe for plundering.'

He smiled down at the girl by his side.

'I will relate to you a tale of a rich king and a cruel step-mother – of a beautiful princess and a banished prince.'

There was a concerted cheer and rush for the cantina. Soon the street was empty but for the bloodied corpse of Morales.

The first dog appeared and cautiously approached, the smell of fresh blood bringing drooling saliva to its mouth.

# 21

Leo Postlewaite preened himself in the mirror and admired the dark growth of hair on his face. He angled his youthful and handsome face in an attempt to view the vicious scar along his jaw inflicted by the bandit leader, Ignacio.

'Mmmm. . . .'

He was still unsure if the beard suited him but he liked even less the idea of the ugly scar being exposed. The doctor had removed the stitches, grumbling as he did so.

'Hell, young fella, I sure hope the next time I attend you I won't be pulling lead out of you instead of goddamn stitches.'

Leo, by now used to the grumbling sawbones, said nothing. He had been dreading having the stitches removed but found the experience not as bad as he had imagined.

'There you go. Patched up and ready for more blades and guns to shred your guileless young body.'

'Thanks, Doc. What do I owe you?'

'You owe me a drink down at the Silver Penny next time you catch me in there. Now get along with you.'

Leo had found lodgings with a bustling widow-woman and her three daughters. The oldest girl was twelve and along with her younger sisters dreamed of walking the handsome young deputy up the aisle of the local church. Their mother was also eyeing her young lodger with more than matronly interest.

Leo, blissfully unaware of the fluttering he was causing in this particular batch of female hearts, finished his toilet and left his room.

'Morning, Mr Postlewaite.'

A row of earnest, freshly scrubbed young faces greeted him.

'Morning, girls,' Leo returned, smiling broadly. 'My, I never did see a finer set of young women in the whole of Texas. It sure makes a man glad to be alive to see such a row of purty young faces.'

Grabbing his hat, Leo exited the boarding-house, completely unaware of the four pair of eyes that followed him till he disappeared from sight.

'Morning, Phil,' Leo greeted his boss, as he walked into the law office.

'Leo,' Sheriff Morgan mumbled, preoccupied with studying some papers on his desk. He held out a telegraph message.

'What do you make of that?'

'Request inform when officers Grover and Perry due to deliver prisoner Ignacio.' Leo read out. He frowned. 'When did this come in?'

'This morning – you know what this means?'

Thoughtfully, Leo replaced the paper on the desk.

'What you reckon?'

'It means that Ignacio has once again escaped the gallows. My guess it that someone ambushed Grover and Perry and rescued our friend Ignacio. If you ask me he is safely holed up in his den planning more devilry.'

Sheriff Morgan leaned back in his chair and gazed soberly at his young deputy.

'We'll have to go out and look for them two idiots. They are two damn fools but I would hate to think of them stranded out there somewhere or even worse. The sooner we start the better.'

He stood up and reached for his hat.

'Come on, let's get started.'

They camped that night in a dry wash. There was little conversation as they settled down.

'We'll make an early start.' The bearded sheriff stared off into the night. 'I got a bad feeling about this. If them marshals is still alive. . . .' He left the statement unfinished.

Next morning they were up at first light. They breakfasted on biscuits and coffee before saddling up and continuing the search. The track from Denton to Houston was not a busy one and they met no other travellers. As they rode the men kept a lookout out for any signs of riders leaving the main trail.

'They'da made at least one overnight stop.' Morgan commented.

The land stretched out vast and measureless. Heat-haze simmered on the horizon. It seemed to the two lawmen they were on a hopeless search. It was around noon before they got indications of something unusual.

They were passing a hollow that was filled with low growing shrub and small stunted trees when the horses became skittish.

'Whoa there.'

Both riders leaned down, stroking their mounts and eyeing the undergrowth.

'Something's spooking these horses. Hold the reins, Leo, while I go take a look. Might be an animal or something that's frightening them.'

As soon as he entered the undergrowth Sheriff Morgan could smell it.

'Something dead in here,' he called, 'it stinks.'

A few minutes later he called again. 'Tie up them horses and come on in here, Leo.'

There was not much of the bodies left. Scavengers had nibbled and torn at the carcasses. Someone had gone to the trouble of staking the men out. Rawhide still held dead wrists to the wooden pegs that had been fashioned from tree branches.

'Son of a bitch, he wasn't content with just killing them. It looks as if they were tortured.'

Leo gazed with horrified fascination at the staked figures on the ground. He had certainly not liked the two marshals but he would never in his wildest imaginings have wished anything like this to happen to them.

They searched the area but found nothing more.

'No horses, no weapons – they took anything of use. We can't leave them here. I guess we'll have to figure out a way of getting them back to Denton. They deserve a decent burial at least.'

In the end it was Leo who suggested the Indian method of transport. They fashioned a couple of travois using ropes and branches cut from the trees. It was a gruesome task to free the cadavers from the bonds that had held them in their last terrible hours. They wrapped the remains in blankets and fastened the grisly bundles behind the horses. The combination of having to drag the unusual carts with the cadavers made the task of riding the frightened horses arduous. It was a fraught journey back to Denton for both men and animals.

'You take them straight to the undertaker's, Leo. I'll go down the telegraph office and send word to Houston. The sooner they know what's happened the better. See you back at the office.'

When Leo walked into the sheriff's office, Phil Morgan looked at him with a sober expression.

'It looks as if you might be right about your suspicions

regarding Victoria McQueen.' As he spoke, he handed Leo another telegram. 'Take a look at that.'

Leo read the wire. 'It says here they're sending a man to follow up the lead on Bernice Quartermain. He's coming down here to speak to me first.'

Morgan eyed his deputy shrewdly – seeing the worry in the young man's face.

'Hell, Leo, stop worrying about your former employer. We got enough on our plates with Ignacio on the loose.'

Leo rubbed a hand wearily across his face.

'I guess you're right, Phil. Things've sure been hectic since I arrived in Denton. I guess I'll have to view my life in two bits – as that before Denton and post Denton. I sure as hell wish I was back at Pentland and all since had never happened.'

'Go on, take the rest of the night off,' Morgan responded, seeing how weary his young deputy looked. 'I guess seeing them two bodies out there knocked the starch outa you.'

Leo gave a wry grimace and taking the sheriff at his word left the office and headed down towards the Silver Penny. What he needed right now was a stiff drink. Sheriff Morgan was right. Seeing the tortured bodies of Grover and Perry had jolted him. Prior to that he had not realized men could be so sadistic. Not a killer by instinct, he now wished he had managed to kill Ignacio instead of bringing him in to face trial.

'I sure as hell won't make that mistake again,' he muttered.

The flash and bang of the pistol from the alleyway snapped his head up. At the same time something punched him and he was falling.

## 22

Ignacio sat his horse in front of his men. They were a villainous looking gang of desperados festooned with bandoleers stuffed full of ammunition. There were about two-dozen men in the group and they looked a pretty formidable force.

'Jose and Pedro – ride into this town that is called Ladler. Find out what you can about the local law. I want the rest of you to break up into small groups and scout out the country – especially around this Ranchero Pentland. Try and find out where they are holding the big herds and the best trails to take them south when we round them up. Make special note of numbers of *vaqueros* with the cattle. If all goes according to plan we will strip this ranchero and become very rich men.

'And stay out of trouble. No getting drunk and no fighting with the local cowboys. *Adios*, my friends, and good hunting.'

The bandit chief flicked back his jacket to expose a marshal's badge pinned to his woollen shirt. He grinned at his men.

'I go to meet a beautiful heiress.'

He swept this arm in an encompassing circle.

'We will meet back here in two days' time. Try to look like a posse assembling to apprehend a bunch of Mexican bandits we believe are heading into this part of the country.'

This last observation drew whoops of mirth from his men. Smiling broadly, Ignacio waved his arm in farewell and watched his gang as they dispersed to their various tasks.

'Broderick.'

The young cowboy heard Imogen call out his name and turned with a smile on his face. His cheerful countenance in no way matched the worried frown on the face of the beautiful, dark-haired young girl hurrying up to him.

'Have you heard from Leo?' she asked anxiously.

Broderick nodded, pursing his lips at the same time.

'Yes, miss, got a letter a few days ago.'

'Oh Broderick, you should have come to me straight-away. You know I'm worried about Leo.'

'I . . . I been busy, Miss Imogen, I guess that's why I never did.'

'Did he reply to my letter? Oh, Broderick. Let me have it. I can't wait.'

'Miss Imogen,' Broderick shifted his feet uncomfort-ably, 'there weren't nothing in the envelope but a letter to me.'

Imogen stared at him, shaking her head slowly.

'Surely you must be mistaken. You did send my letter with yours?'

'Sure did, miss, I folded it up and put it in with what I wrote telling him all the news and saying as how we all miss him.'

Imogen stared at the cowboy, a slight frown on her normally smooth forehead. Broderick's heart ached to see the distress in the young girl's eyes.

'You're telling me he wrote to you but not to me,' she said in a low voice.

'He . . . he's probably finding it hard to write to you, Miss Imogen, what with being separated from you and all

101

. . . He's probably too much eat up with grief. . . .'

She stared anxiously back at him.

'You think so?'

'Why sure, miss, he ain't never been away from home before. He'd be all homesick and yearning for you and in too much heartache to write to someone as he loves.'

'Oh, Broderick, maybe what you say is true. But tell me what he wrote to you.'

Relieved that his efforts to mollify the girl's feelings were successful, the cowboy took an envelope from his pocket and handed it to her.

'I can do better, miss, why don't you read it for yourself. Read it out loud to me so as I can remember it all over again.'

'*Some strange things have happened to me since arriving here in Denton on a wet night some time ago,*' she read out. '*I helped out the local sheriff – a fella the name of Phil Morgan. He took me on as deputy and we went after a notorious gang and brung back the leader Ignacio. Tell everyone I miss them very much. Maybe when things are not so hectic here in Denton I'll come on a visit. Your old buddy, Leo.*'

When she finished reading the girl read it again, this time silently mouthing the words. When she finished she looked up at her companion.

'He . . . he never mentions me, Broderick.'

'He'll write to you, Miss Imogen, don't you fret about that. I know Leo will never forget you.'

But, as she walked away, the young cowboy could see the dejected slump to the girl's shoulders.

'Goddamn you, Leo, why don't you write to Miss Imogen?' he muttered. 'I can tell she sure as hell is all bust up inside from missing you. What the hell's he playing at?'

Before she got to the house a rider entered the yard.

The cowhand and the girl looked with some curiosity at the stranger. He wore a tall hat and a duster coat. Beneath the hat his face was bronzed and roguish. He doffed the hat when he saw the girl staring up at him. In doing so he exposed a shock of pale-gold hair. Imogen stared at that scarred but handsome face and felt strangely attracted.

'Good afternoon.'

The newcomer flicked aside his coat to reveal a badge.

'Marshal Tom Grover at your service. I have a message for a Miss Imogen Breen. Can you tell me where I can find her?'

'I'm Imogen Breen. What message is this?'

'With your permission, miss.'

The stranger smiled down at her and alighted.

'I been riding for some days now.'

'Oh, I am sorry. It is remiss of me. Come inside, Marshal, and I will order refreshments. Broderick will see to your horse.'

She ushered him into the house. On the way through she met Victoria McQueen.

Victoria eyed up the tall, bronzed man with the scarred face with more than a passing interest.

'Who's your guest?' she asked, as she smiled coquettishly at the stranger.

'Ma'am.' He nodded courteously to the older woman.

'Mrs McQueen, be a darling and order coffee from the kitchen.'

Imogen steered her guest into the morning-room, neatly sidestepping the woman's curiosity.

Victoria McQueen stared balefully at the closed door. Instead of complying with Imogen's request she walked out onto the veranda and stationed herself outside the window of the morning-room. She could hear every word spoken inside.

'You say you have a message for me, Marshal?'

That handsome, scarred face smiled, exposing even white teeth. He glanced around the room.

'We are alone, miss?'

'Of course, why do you ask?'

'The message I have is for your ears only. I was told to speak to no one else.'

'Goodness, you have my curiosity stirred with all this secrecy. I can assure you we are alone and not likely to be overheard.'

Fixing her with his unique, pale-blue eyes the stranger nodded.

'Good enough. The reason for all this secrecy is that Leo Postlewaite sent me.'

Imogen's eyes opened wide.

'Leo, is he all right?'

'Oh yes, miss,' Ignacio reassured her. 'He's a lawman now. Him and I are on a mission. I'm afraid I can't tell you what it is because of security, but he asked me to come here and arrange a meeting between you pair. He wants to ask you a favour.'

'Is Leo here? Oh, tell me where he is! I'll do whatever he asks.'

'Whoa there, miss.' Ignacio held up a hand. 'You ain't heard what it is he wants. He told me some garbled tale that he wasn't welcome here and that you and he would have to meet in secret. The mission we're on involves pretending to be wealthy cattle buyers and we need a lot of cash to carry out the deception. He was wondering if you could help out in this respect and loan us the money so we can complete the job and bag our villains. The money will be safe enough. It won't ever leave our possession. We just need to flash it around. When the job's done we'll return your money and perhaps the government might just toss in a little bonus for all your help in this matter.'

'Oh, Marshal Grover, just tell me what to do and I'll be only too happy to help.'

# 23

The bullet clipped his shoulder and spun him round. The second one missed him as he fell to the boardwalk. Even as he hit the boards Leo rolled towards the roadway and fell from the walkway. In spite of the shock and surprise of the sudden attack his gun was in his hand and he fired instinctively towards the shadowy figure.

He was able to aim at the bushwhacker for the man was still shooting at him. Leo saw the man outlined in the gun flashes and put two bullets into the target. Even with the disadvantage of lying on the ground Leo knew at that distance he could not miss. The man screamed and staggered back. Leo heard the thud as the gun in the man's hand slipped out of his grasp. He held his fire as he watched the shadowy figure slump to the ground. Cautiously he rose to his feet, keeping his Colt pointed at the moaning figure in the alley.

'Don't do anything sudden,' he called. 'I got three more bullets here for your worthless carcass.'

The man made no reply, or if he did it was lost somewhere amidst his groans. Leo saw the gun the would-be assassin had dropped and he kicked it out of reach.

Behind him in the street he could hear men calling.

'Over here,' he yelled. 'I got me a bushwhacker.'

Then Sheriff Morgan arrived and took charge.

'You all right, Leo?'

'Caught me a bullet in the shoulder.'

Leo put his hand up and felt the wetness on his shirt.

'I think the goddamn skunk ruined my shirt.'

'Let's take a look at him.'

Sheriff Morgan pulled the wounded man over none too gently to peer into his face.

'Well I'll be damned – it's Jason, the fella from the livery.'

Leo stopped feeling at his shoulder to stare at the man on the ground.

'Help me, Jesus you gotta help,' the wounded man pleaded. 'I'm dying. Oh please help me.'

'Well I'll be. . . .' Leo trailed off, puzzled by this new development.

'You men,' Morgan collared two onlookers. 'Help me carry this halfwit down the sawbones.'


It was early morning before the two lawmen could confer. Leo's arm was in a sling. He felt the sling was unnecessary for apart for a soreness in his shoulder where the bullet had taken some flesh he could move his arm without discomfort. But the tetchy doc had insisted and rather than argue with the old man Leo felt it was easier to comply with his instructions and promised to wear the sling.

'Now we know the identity of Ignacio's spy in town,' the sheriff stated, wearily rubbing a hand across his face. 'Come to think on it, it was the perfect cover. The livery hired out horses and wagons so he was first to know when goods and gold was being transported. Then he passed the information to the gang and was paid for his troubles.' He shook his head. 'He sure had everyone fooled. We all thought the fella was an idiot. Just goes to show you can't take anyone for granted.'

He gazed speculatively at his deputy.

'Leo, maybe this job ain't the right one for you. Since joining up you've had more than your fair share of shootings and stabbings, not to mention a fight with a jealous boyfriend.'

Leo stared back at the sheriff.

'Maybe you're right, Phil. I guess cow-punching is a mite less dangerous. In that job you only stand the chance of being thrown by a maverick horse, or gored by an angry steer, or trampled to death in a stampede, or getting killed in a shootout with rustlers.'

He was pleased to see the slight alarm in Sheriff Morgan's eyes as he finished.

'Maybe it's time to ask for a raise in my wages.'

A slow grin crossed the sheriff's face as he realized the youngster was teasing him.

'Wages – what wages? It's all gone on medical bills.'

He yawned prodigiously.

'Anyway it's time we both had some sleep. And mind how you go,' he added as Leo stood up. 'This time try not to get stabbed or shot on your way to the rooming-house.'

Back at his lodgings the females fussed round him vying with each other to please him. It took some persuading on his part to assure his four admirers that in spite of the sling and bandaged shoulder he was not seriously hurt. When he finally got to his bed he fell into a deep and dreamless sleep.

It was well into the afternoon when he surfaced. His shoulder ached some but he felt refreshed and exceedingly hungry.

'Um,' he mused, 'I guess I missed lunch, but maybe they can rustle me up a sandwich.'

To his surprise and gratification when he asked for a snack he was treated to a full three-course meal.

While the lady of the house laboured at the stove her three daughters served at the table avidly watching their lodger's every move. When he reached for the salt three small hands darted to the pot to push it closer to him. Each time his coffee cup emptied there was a concerted rush to the stove to replenish it. The coffee was creamed and sugared for him. Biscuits were buttered in anticipation of his need. Three pairs of eyes followed the food from the plate to his mouth. Leo at first was amused by all the attention he was receiving and then began to feel embarrassed as the youngsters edged closer and closer to him. At last he sat back from the table with a hearty sigh.

'I do declare that was the best meal it was ever my pleasure to eat. I think I'll just go right out and get shot again if that's the treatment I'll be getting.'

The alarm in the faces of the three youngsters was comic to see and Leo was hard put not to laugh out loud.

'Oh, Mr Postlewaite, you do take care. You would do well to give up that dangerous job,' his landlady declared. 'Get a nice safe position in a store, or bank, or something.'

Full to bursting Leo stood up from the table.

'I'm sure tempted to take your advice. For now I guess I'd better report for duty down at the sheriff's office.'

He was followed to the front door and to his great embarrassment the eldest girl burst into tears as he left.

Puzzling the strange behaviour of small girls Leo walked through the town. This time he cautiously watched out for lurking gunmen and assassins. When he arrived at his destination he found a stranger seated in the office with Sheriff Morgan.

'Howdy, young fella, how you feeling?'

'Much better now I've had a sleep and a feed.'

Leo nodded to the stranger.

'Leo, this is Arthur Keller. Houston sent him down to see you. We've been waiting for you to surface. I told him what a lazy sonabitch you were and we probably wouldn't see you till Sunday.'

Keller grinned at Leo.

'Howdy, Leo, I take no notice of this old grump. Him and I go back a long way. Saved my life once. Never did get to repay him.'

They shook hands and Leo took stock of the lawman.

In the same age group as Morgan, he was tall and muscular with broad shoulders. He had a well-groomed moustache and was very tidy in his dress.

'The long and short of it, Leo, is we think you may have given us a lead on this woman, Bernice Quartermain. We've been after her for some time. But by the time relatives of her victims alert us she's fled the scene. Your wire regarding your suspicions of this Victoria McQueen puts us ahead of the game. What I want is for you to accompany me to where she's at and help us entrap her before she commits any more crimes.'

Leo blinked in surprise.

'I sure would like to help you, Marshal, but I ain't exactly welcome at Pentland.'

Keller nodded agreeably.

'All the better. While you're getting yourself entangled in whatever situation arises it'll more 'an likely distract the woman from our real purpose.'

'Keller,' interrupted Sheriff Morgan, 'you serious about repaying that debt you reckon you owe me?'

'Hell, Morgan, you know I'd go to hell and back again for you.'

'How's about you and me swap jobs for a week or two. You sit in this office and take care of the citizens of Denton and I go up to Ladler with my deputy.'

Keller frowned at the sheriff.

'You serious, Phil?'

Morgan nodded solemnly.

'I kinda feel responsible for this young hellion. Since he's been my deputy he's been stabbed, stomped and shot. I think I act like a good luck charm keeping him alive.'

Keller started to laugh then. He laughed so hard he had to sit down again.

'Morgan,' he at last managed to gasp, 'only you could twist logic around like that.'

The men grinned at each other across the office.

'Go on, you old warhorse, if anyone can keep him alive you can.'

## 24

The ranch house stood in a low-sided valley. There was a house, three barns and a stable at the side of a corral. It was obvious that many years had passed since it had been occupied. An aura of desolation hung about the buildings. The roofs of the barns had long ago caved in and doors sagged on broken hinges.

Ignacio spotted the rider coming from the direction of Pentland. After satisfying himself it was the girl and she was alone he put away his glass and nudged his horse down towards the derelict house. He was waiting for the Breen girl when she rode into the yard of the abandoned ranch.

'Miss Breen, I can see Leo had very good reason to believe you could be trusted to help him.'

Imogen glanced around the yard.

'Are you alone? I thought Leo was to come with you.'

'Yeah, it was a last-minute hitch. He had to stay back at the camp. We'd arranged to meet someone and they didn't turn up so he's had to wait in case they were just delayed or something.'

Ignacio suddenly smiled in his engaging roguish manner and Imogen felt she could forgive this likeable rogue anything.

'We drew lots as to who should stay and who would make the rendezvous with you.'

His gaze was drawn to he saddle-bags draped on the girl's mount.

'You manage to bring any money with you?'

She looked down and patted the saddle-bags then frowned.

'I was never so scared in all my life. Pa keeps cash in his safe to pay the hands and buy stock. I had to wait till he was out of the way before attempting anything. I don't know how much there is but at a rough guess there's ten thousand at least.'

Ignacio whistled in admiration.

'Your pa must be a very rich man to keep that much in petty cash. I suppose he keeps the bulk of his wealth in the bank.'

'I suppose. I never had to bother much about money. Pa was always generous with me.'

Her face clouded somewhat.

'Though now he seems to be spending a lot on Victoria McQueen.'

Ignacio raised his eyebrows.

'I take it from your expression you don't cotton to this McQueen.'

'Oh no, don't get me wrong, she's very nice and is always asking after my welfare but there is just that something that seems a bit insincere about her.' Suddenly she laughed. 'I'm sure you don't want to hear all these domestic details, Marshal Grover. You and Leo have more important things to worry about than me and my imagined likes and dislikes.'

His smile reassured her he was not in the least bothered by her gossip.

'Miss, I could stay here all day and chat to you – but duty calls.'

He gestured towards the saddle-bags.

'Can I take charge of that? When I get a chance to count it I'll make you out an official receipt for the full amount.'

Imogen immediately pulled the saddle-bags and handed them over.

'Marshal Grover, when will I get to meet Leo?'

That roguish grin was on his face as he answered. 'Why don't you ride back to camp with me and give Leo a nice surprise? While you and he get reacquainted I'll count the money, make out a receipt and then he can escort you back home.'

'Oh, Marshal, if only I could.'

'That's settled then. I guess I'm getting to be right romantic in my old age. Let's go.'

There was a movement by the house. Both Ignacio and Imogen turned to stare at the man exiting the broken front door.

'How touching – the daughter stealing from her father.

Old Cyrus won't be too pleased when he discovers it was his daughter who stole the money to give to her banished lover.'

'Claude, how did you get here?'

He stood there with an open sneer on his coarse face. In his hand he held a Colt. He was pointing it at Ignacio. Two more men appeared from round the corner of the house. They also had pistols pointed towards the couple in the yard. Imogen's lips tightened as she stared at the man she despised.

'Just climb down off them horses. We got a lot to discuss.'

'Hang fire there, fella,' Ignacio drawled. 'You don't know what you're getting into.'

Ignacio drew back his coat and revealed the marshal's badge.

'I'm a United States Marshal. If you interfere in this matter you'll have to answer to the courts.'

'Yeah, and who's gonna tell them?'

Ignacio frowned. 'What you saying, fella? I'm the law here. You go up against me you go up against the full force of the law. You'll have a price on your head and be hunted down. No one messes with a duly appointed marshal, not if they got any sense.'

'The way I see it, Marshal, you and that loser Postlewaite lured this poor girl to this isolated farmhouse with some cock and bull story to gain her trust. Then you and your accomplice robbed her. It's not me the authorities will be hunting, it'll be you and Postlewaite. Now just toss down that bag of money and any weapons you might be carry-ing. Shoot the son of a bitch if he tries anything funny,' he said to his two accomplices.

Reluctantly Ignacio let the saddle-bags drop. Carefully he plucked the Peacemaker from his holster and it followed the money.

'You're making a big mistake, fella. I'd quit while I was ahead if I was you.'

'Well you ain't me, you sad-assed cretin. Now climb down both of you and we'll go inside this mansion.'

There was nothing for it but to comply.

Claude, a triumphant leer on his face, motioned the couple towards the door of the ruined house. The inside was just as derelict as the outside with stains where rain had leaked and large dusty cobwebs and broken floors.

'Take the marshal through there.'

Claude pointed with his pistol towards a room that may have been a kitchen, for the rusty remains of a stove could be seen.

'Keep your pistols on him at all times. If he tries anything just shoot him. If you don't want to kill him just shoot him in the leg or somewhere, to slow him down. Don't worry about him being a lawman. From what I know of lawmen they're all corrupt.'

The two gunmen prodded Ignacio towards the kitchen. Claude leered at Imogen.

'In there.' He pointed to a door. 'You and I have a little business to sort out.'

'The only business I have with you is for me to tell you how sorry you'll be when my father finds out you been holding me against my will. He won't take kindly to having his daughter held up at gunpoint and robbed. He'll throw you off the ranch so fast you'll land in jail without your feet touching the ground.'

'Is that a fact?'

Claude pushed the girl through a doorway into a large room that was empty except for a few broken sticks of furniture. The sneer he gave Imogen was loaded with intent.

'You recognize these clothes?' he asked, waving the barrel of the pistol up and down in front of his person.

Imogen frowned and shook her head.

'No, why should I?'

'Before I came out here to wait for you I went into your precious Leo's room and found some of his clothes hanging in the closet.'

Still frowning, Imogen stared at the garments. Claude was wearing a pair of navy-blue serge trousers and a heavy twill shirt of an indiscriminate beige colour.

'Even if they are Leo's old clothes you still look like a clown in them,' she said, her voice dripping with contempt.

Unfazed by her comments Claude continued, 'You told me once you preferred Postlewaite's dirty laundry to me. Well, now you get both. While I pleasure you dressed in these clothes, you can imagine it's your goddamn Leo on top of you.'

'You worm – you wouldn't dare touch me. My father would horsewhip you before hanging you from the nearest tree.'

'We'll see about that, my dear. How will Breen find out if there are no witnesses to the deed? No one ever comes out here. It'll be months before they find you and the lawman. They'll figure you and the marshal were having a lover's tryst and Postlewaite found you together and in a rage of jealousy he killed you both. In the meantime I'll be enjoying that ten thousand you so thoughtfully provided. I couldn't have dreamed up the whole thing if I tried. I get to pay you back for all those insults and ten thousand dollars into the bargain. So prepare yourself, Miss High and Mighty. Your love life begins and ends here in this dirty old house.'

'You're mad. You're a raving lunatic. Let me go now and you may escape the worst.'

But even as she spoke, Claude McQueen lurched towards her, a leer on his brute face.

## 25

'Have you ever seen a man hang?'

The two gunmen took a quick look at each other but other than that exchange of glances made no other response.

'I'm only asking in case you don't realize what you got yourselves into.'

Ignacio stared speculatively at the two men. One was in his middle years with a clipped grey moustache and folds of sagging skin under his eyes. The other was much younger with a round bland face. His eyes were small and pig-like and he had a pallid complexion as if he spent too much time in smoky saloon bars and not enough time in the fresh air.

'I've seen too many men hang. It's a dirty business watching them jerk out their lives in the end of a rope. It might be me as has to do the hanging if the official hang-man can't get in time. I hate that part of the job. You see, the proper executioner has skills that inexperienced fellas like me lack. He knows just how to place the hanging knot so as the neck breaks as the body falls through the trap.

'I once had to hang a fella down in Austin. I put the rope round his neck and opened the trap. He went down and I thought my job was done. Then dang me if there was this noise coming from the hole where he had gone through. I looked down and there he was kicking and

116

gasping as the rope slowly strangled him. I can tell you fellas, I was terrified.'

Ignacio shook his head at the memory.

'Then the judge shouted, "Tom, get down there and swing on his legs". Well I just gawked at the judge. "Climb down and yank on his boots to finish him off", he yelled again. I can tell you the sweat was pouring off me like an autumn shower. And all the time that fella was slowly strangulating. I had to clamber down underneath the gallows and grab him by the boots and pull like blazes. I can tell you it was a filthy job all right. That fella had pissed and shit his pants. I had nightmares for weeks after that.'

Ignacio pulled at the collar of his shirt.

'Damn me, I break into a sweat just to talk about it.'

'Shut up, we don't want to hear no more!'

'No, I don't suppose you do. They say a man gets an erection as he drops down that hole.'

Ignacio shivered at the thought.

'Can you imagine that? You get a stiffener on and that there noose chokes you off. What a filthy business!'

'Mister, if you don't shut up, I'll put a slug in you.'

'I ain't meaning no offence, fella. I just thought you might like to know how it was to be hanged seeing as you two are headed down that road.'

The gunmen glanced uneasily at each other.

'We ain't going to no hanging.'

'Maybe not. McQueen might just have you killed. You see he can't afford to have no witness to murder.'

'Murder – what the hell you mean murder?'

'You think he's gonna let that girl live after today? He's in there now raping her. Then he'll kill her to shut her up.'

As if to emphasize his claim, at that precise moment a

woman's scream rang out. Startled the men looked at each other.

'Hell, I didn't sign up to no murder.'

'Then he'll have to kill me to keep me from coming after him,' Ignacio continued remorselessly. 'When a US Marshal is murdered the forces of law and order leave no stone unturned to track down his killers. You fellas are sure dang fired heading for the gallows.'

'Ben, I don't want no part of this,' the younger of the gunmen said. 'I'm for getting out while we can. But what're we gonna do with this lawman?'

'Look,' Ignacio said reasonably as another scream rang out, 'you fellas ain't committed no crime as yet. You give me back my gun and when you leave, as far as I'm concerned, you ride out of here with a clean slate.'

'Hell, Billy, he's right. We're putting our heads in a noose for a lousy fifty dollars. Mister, I'm putting your gun on the floor here. Just you keep your side of the bargain.'

'A very wise decision, fellas,' Ignacio said. 'I just want one favour from you and we're evens.'

He fished out an envelope from an inside pocket

'Can you deliver this letter to someone from Pentland? It's addressed to Cyrus Breen, the owner. But you don't have to give it to him personally.'

'Sure, Marshal.'

Ben grabbed the proffered envelope and almost ran from the room with his partner hard on his heels. Ignacio picked up his Peacemaker and then turned to seek out Imogen.

Claude was sitting on top of the girl. Her blouse was ripped exposing her shoulders and the tops of her breasts. The young man's face was red with anger. He drew back his arm and backhanded Imogen. Her hair was mussed and her face bruised where he had hit her several times to subdue her. Ignacio stood in the doorway and regarded the uneven struggle between the young girl and her burly attacker.

In spite of the battering she was receiving Imogen was pluckily fighting back. Her teeth were gritted and she struggled unceasingly against the heavily muscled man sitting astride her. It was going to be no easy conquest for Claude.

He was used to the compliant whores whose time he bought and who were forced to endure his cruel practices out of necessity. Now he had his hands full with a girl of fire and spirit fighting back. It disconcerted him and indeed frightened him not a little.

In desperation he bunched his fist and smashed it down on the girl's upturned face. Imogen cried out and blood spurted from her busted nose. She ceased struggling temporarily and Claude grunted in satisfaction. He raised his fist again to repeat his vicious punch but never got to land it.

Someone seized him by the hair and brutally yanked him backwards.

'Goddamn it,' he screamed, as he was hauled by his hair across the floor.

Ineffectually he grappled with the hand, so painfully gripping him. It was hopeless. He was dragged across the filthy floor and his screams were an echo of the girl's screams as she had fought him but a short time ago. His head slammed against the far wall and the grip on his hair was released. Dazedly he blinked up at the tall figure of the bogus marshal.

'Claude, Claude, Claude, what on earth are we going to do with you?' Ignacio shook his head in mock exasperation. 'You are a disgrace to your manhood. I had to kill another sonabitch just like you last week. Morales thought it was fun to beat up females. He had his throat cut. The fairer sex ain't as strong as us males. We oughta protect them – not batter them.'

He turned to look across at Imogen. She was sitting up wiping at the blood on her face. When she saw him looking she suddenly realized the state of her torn blouse and, blushing deeply, began to cover up.

Seeing the marshal distracted Claude went for his gun. Ignacio swivelled with the grace of a dancer and kicked him in the face. Claude's head banged back on the wall again and blood began streaming from his nose.

'Goddamn!' he screamed. 'You're dead fella – dead and buried.'

His face was creased in pain as he gingerly massaged the back of his head. Ignacio reached down and plucked the pistol from Claude's holster. He turned and walked across to Imogen and handed her the weapon.

'You wanna put a slug in that excuse for a human being?'

Imogen looked at the pistol and then looked in surprise at the marshal whom she supposed should stick to doing things in a lawful manner. She shuddered.

'No thanks, my pa will take care of him.'

She looked with some contempt at the moaning figure crouched against the far wall.

'He wore Leo's clothing thinking it would make him more attractive to me. He's a hateful, cruel beast!'

Ignacio nodded in understanding.

'Take the saddle-bags outside and wait for me there. I'll bind this fella so as he won't be able to come after us. I'll send word to the sheriff in Ladler to come and get him.'

Left alone, the two men stared at each other. Claude's face was filled with hate for the man who had interrupted his lustful revenge. He was rubbing the back of his head with one hand while attempting to stem the flow of blood from his nose with the other. Ignacio crouched before the injured man. In his hand he held a long slim stiletto.

'I wish I had time to spend with you, my friend. My speciality is slicing bits off fellas and listening to their screams. It fascinates me how much agony the human body can take before expiring. Every man is different in that respect. You look a strong young fella. My guess it that you'd give me much pleasure.' Ignacio sighed. 'But that is now pure speculation.'

'Go to hell, you bastard! We'll meet again, and next time it'll be you'll die screaming.'

'Indeed I may go to hell, but not just yet. You'll just have to go ahead of me.'

The strike was swift and sure. The slim blade plunged into Claude's chest. His eyes opened wide and he stared with incomprehension at the knifeman. Then his mouth opened as if he would protest at the summary way his captor had treated him. But the steel that had pierced his heart had fatally damaged it. With a long sigh, the eyes clouded over and the body sagged back against the wall.

Ignacio withdrew the blade and wiped it on his victim. Then he stood and walked outside to the waiting girl.

## 26

'There she is, Pentland, the biggest spread in Texas.'

There was a hint of pride in Leo's voice as he spoke. Sheriff Morgan eased himself in the saddle and gazed out across the vast stretches of grasslands. There was nothing to break the view until somewhere in the hazy distance land and sky merged.

'Hell, all I can see is grass and cattle.'

'Yessiree.'

Leo hooked his leg over his saddle horn and the two riders sat their mounts each sunk in their own thoughts.

This was nostalgic homecoming for Leo. There were even the familiar sights and sounds of cattle being herded up towards them. Leo frowned.

'That's funny, they shouldn't be moving cattle now. The herds need to be closer to home range. Even Claude should know that and if he don't then Cyrus would put him right.'

'Maybe they're for market,' Morgan opined.

'When we sell beef it usually goes north. These fellas are pushing them south. I'll just mosey down there and try and find out what's going on.'

Leo nudged his horse towards the herd. He estimated there was several hundred head with four or five cowhands hazing them along.

Morgan shook his head. 'We're lawmen not cowboys,' he called after Leo's retreating back.

But his young deputy made no reply and Sheriff Morgan, muttering under his breath, was forced to follow.

As he approached the cowboys Leo was even more puzzled as he saw the riders were not dressed Texas style but in the manner of *vaqueros*. The herders appeared to take no notice of Leo but kept the steers moving.

Cattle bellowed as they milled along – like all Texas longhorns, ornery enough to protest at any restrictions on their freedom. A group of four managed to elude the herders and broke away from the main bunch.

Instinctively Leo kicked his horse into motion and rode

to cut them off. He hassled the cattle back in the direction of their fellows but was surprised to see none of the *vaqueros* seemed to have noticed the breakaway. Leo's four plunged back into the main herd. His good turn done he rode towards the nearest rider.

'Howdy,' he called out, 'where you headed?'

As he drew nearer, Leo could see the man was heavily armed. He began to suspect something was not quite right. The rider he had greeted shook his head and waved Leo away. When this had no effect he suddenly drew his pistol.

'Vamoose, gringo, or I shoot.'

'The hell you will, fella.'

Leo grabbed for his own weapon.

The shot cracked out loud and startling above the sounds of the cattle. Leo ducked instinctively but had no idea if the shot had come near. By now his own gun was in his hand and he fired over the *vaquero*'s head.

'Hold your fire, you goddamn lobo!' he yelled.

The gunman ignored his order and loosed off another shot but his mount was jumpy and again Leo could not tell where the bullet went.

The cattle began to mill about now, startled by the loud reports.

Sheriff Morgan, seeing his deputy under threat, unsheathed his Winchester and the heavier report of the rifle added to the confusion of noise. The leading steers, made nervous by the sudden explosion of gunfire, surged forward and within moments a full-scale stampede was started. All Leo could do was watch in some dismay as the herd gathered momentum.

The *vaquero*, seeing he now had two gringos to deal with, put spurs to his mount and followed the runaway steers. Instinctively, Leo kicked his heels into the flanks of his own mount and gave chase. Behind him came Sheriff Morgan.

The young lawman was outraged by the behaviour of the *vaquero*. By now he realized he had come upon a gang of rustlers. He holstered his gun and concentrated on the chase.

His quarry was flogging his pony mercilessly to get away from Leo and follow the stampeding steers. Relentlessly the young lawman was closing the gap between them. With the herd running past them the other herders were following but they were edging their mounts in behind the fleeing cattle with the obvious intent of coming to the aid of their besieged comrade.

The *vaquero* cast a glance behind. Seeing Leo pursuing him, the fleeing bandit flung a few shots at him. Leo did not flinch knowing it would be a very lucky shot that would score a hit from the back of a galloping horse. He concentrated on urging his mount to greater speed.

Slowly he was closing the gap. He was mindful of the odds mounting as the other rustlers cut across towards him. Then they had something else to think about for Morgan cut loose with his Winchester.

It was a mad headlong race as the stampeding cattle led the way. With nothing to turn them or stop them Leo mused they could run all the way to the Mexican border and briefly wondered why Mexican rustlers were operating so far north. They usually worked along the border where they could cross the line if things got too hot for them in Texas.

'Come on, my little beauty,' he suddenly yelled at his mount. 'You have the legs of that there mule up ahead.'

It was as if the horse understood the imprecation and gave a sudden surge of speed. Slowly but slowly they closed the gap. With sudden decision Leo loosed his lariat. Like the true cowboy he was he could not bring himself to ride without a rope.

Closer they rode and his target flung a quick look behind. He was not expecting his pursuer to be so close. His gun hand came up and the muzzle was pointed almost in the cowboy's face. As Leo yanked the horse's head to the side and then let fly with his rope he felt the burn of something past his head.

It was a good cast. The loop settled over his quarry's head and Leo kneed his horse at an angle from his victim. Suddenly *vaquero* and horse parted company. Leo looped his end of the rope around his saddle horn as he felt the pull. He jerked on the reins to bring his mount to a stop but could not help dragging the roped bandit. They did not go far for the horse felt the sudden jerk on the rope and hauled up short. Horse and rider were panting from the hasty exertion of the chase. Leo quickly dismounted and ran to his victim.

The unhorsed bandit made no attempt to escape and the young lawman could see the man was winded from his fall. In the excitement of the chase he had forgotten the man's companions. Suddenly shots were whistling all around him. Leo ducked down beside his prisoner and pulled his Colt.

Four riders were bearing down upon him. The shooting faltered as the approaching bandits saw their intended target crouched down beside the winded rustler. Afraid to hit their comrade, they held their fire but kept on coming straight at the young lawman.

The sudden bark of the Winchester startled Leo. He saw one of the bandits throw up his arms and topple from his mount. Sheriff Morgan had dismounted and from somewhere behind Leo fired steadily at the riders.

The large sombrero of one of the oncoming riders was plucked from his head by another shot from Morgan. The bandits pulled up abruptly and slung a few shots towards the rifleman. But pistols were no match against a Winchester.

Leo joined in the shooting and after a moment's hesitation the riders hauled their mounts around and urged them after the stampeding cattle. Leo watched them fleeing and slowly stood up. Sheriff Morgan gathered up the reins of his horse and continued towards Leo.

'It sure as hell beats me how you manage to get involved in all this shooting. I swear if you were on a desert island you'd start a war amongst the apes or whatever species inhabited the dang blasted place.'

Leo grinned ruefully at the sheriff.

'Just doing my job, Sheriff.'

The man at his feet groaned. Leo knelt by his side.

'Let's see what this fella has to say for himself.'

The thunder of hoofs interrupted him. He looked up. A group of horsemen was bearing down on them

'Never a dull moment with you, Post Mortem,' grumbled Sheriff Phil Morgan, as he pulled a handful of cartridges from his pocket and began reloading his Winchester.

# 27

The half-dozen riders pulled up in a swirl of dust. It was obvious from their dress they were the local cowboys. None of them had unlimbered their irons but they circled the two lawmen, hemming them in. Leo kept hold of his rope and eyed up the newcomers.

'This is Pentland range, what the hell you fellas up to?' one of the riders demanded.

'We just tried to stop a bunch of rustlers making off

with them there steers.'

Leo flung a thumb over his shoulder in the direction of the stampeding herd, now a just a dust cloud in the distance.

'I managed to pull this one off his horse and was about to find out where they were taking them. Seems to me you Pentland cowboys are a mite slow when it comes to keeping tabs on stock.'

'How the hell we know you're telling the truth, fella? You might be part of the gang as stopped to help this fella that took a fall from his horse.'

'No wonder rustlers hereabouts have an easy time of it if you boys are an example of Pentland cowboys. How many Pentland riders does it take to catch two innocent fellas as is trying to help?'

'Damn your eyes, fella, we don't take that kind of sass from no dude. If you put those irons away I'll show you what we're made off.'

'Is that so?'

Leo holstered his Colt and handed the rope to Sheriff Morgan.

'Hang on to that there rustler while I teach these fellas a lesson in manners.'

'Post Mortem, have you taken leave of your senses? We ain't here to brawl with cowboys, no matter how sassy.'

Sheriff Morgan was staring at his deputy as if he indeed believed he had gone mad. Leo spat in his hands and rubbed them together before balling them into fists.

'Right, which of you fellas is first, or are you all yella?'

Sheriff Morgan covered his eyes with his hand.

'I can't believe this is happening.'

'You.' Leo pointed to a rider. 'You with the face like a cow's backside, why don't you get down off your horse and try me.'

'Damn your eyes, fella, that does it. I don't take that from no man.'

The cowboy dismounted and handed his reins to a companion to hold. He stalked forward towards Leo.

'Right, Broderick, where do you want me to hit you.'

The cowboy frowned and peered at the bearded stranger who was challenging him to a fight.

'How the hell. . . ?'

Suddenly he gave a whoop and flung himself forward. The two men enfolded each other and swirled around hugging and laughing at the same time while the onlookers watched with some bewilderment.

'Broderick, you son of a bitch. . . .'

'Leo, goddamn Leo, am I glad to see you. Goddamn you, Leo you son of a gun. . . .'

'When you fellas have done kissing and hugging each other can you let a fella know what the hell's going on?'

Sheriff Morgan's laconic voice broke the two friends apart. They were grinning widely and kept their arms draped on each other's shoulders.

'Phil, meet the worst goddamn cowpuncher north of the Rio Grand. Broderick meet Phil Morgan, a very good friend.'

A groan from the Mexican captive brought everyone's attention back to the matter in hand. Sheriff Morgan moved swiftly to disarm the bandit. The man looked up at his captors.

'Gringo trash, why you attack an innocent man?'

'Innocent my foot,' rasped Leo, 'where were you taking those stolen cattle?'

'Stolen! We buy them steers. There is no law against a man driving his own cattle.'

Leo glanced up at his friend.

'You know anything about cattle sales, Broderick?'

'Hell no, Leo, but there's worse things I gotta tell you. Mr Breen received a ransom note yesterday. It's . . . it's . . . Imogen . . . she's been kidnapped. Cyrus Breen brung me in to quiz me when I last seen Imogen and then he told me all about the ransom note. We been out scouring the range for any sign but nothing so far.'

Leo was staring at his friend.

'Imogen kidnapped . . . ransom . . . what the hell you talking about?'

'It's true, Leo. Cyrus showed me the note. He thinks I was the last person to see her.'

'Go on, Broderick, tell me everything.'

Broderick shrugged. 'Like I told Cyrus, a US marshal came to see her about something. Then the next morning Miss Imogen was gone.'

'A US marshal – what'd a US marshal want with Imogen?'

Again the cowboy shrugged. 'I never did find out. I just heard him introduce himself as Marshal Tom Grover. . . .'

He stopped as he saw the startled looks exchanged between Leo and Morgan.

'Ignacio!' Both men spoke the name at the same time. 'Damnation, he took everything from them boys – weapons, horses, badges . . . but what brought him here?'

'You mind that time we had him in the cell, I told you all about Pentland. Never took no mind of him lying there taking in everything. The low-down skulking snake! Now he's come up here and snatched Imogen. Goddamn it, Phil, this is too much. I'm gonna kill that varmint.'

'Not if I get to him first.'

'What the hell you two talking about?' Broderick interrupted the lawmen.

Leo looked warily at the Pentland cowboys.

'Broderick, why don't your boys take after those runaway steers? You stay here with us and we'll fill you in as best we can.'

Once the cowpunchers were on their way Leo told his friend as much as he thought necessary.

'Phil and I here are working for the law only we need to work undercover.' He hesitated a moment before asking. 'How are Cyrus and Mrs McQueen getting along?'

'Real good, I'd say, they were to be married this week.'

Leo and Morgan exchanged glances.

'Broderick, we gotta take you into our confidence. The reason we're here at Pentland is to investigate this Mrs McQueen. We suspect she's some sort of confidence woman who takes advantage of wealthy men. I saw a wanted poster about her and Phil and I were assigned to the case. But goddamn it, this Ignacio business sure complicates things.'

Leo told his friend how Ignacio had murdered the two lawmen and taken on Marshal Grover's identity.

'Somehow he's lured Imogen into his power. Hell, Phil,' Leo turned to his fellow officer. 'I can't take on this McQueen woman while Imogen's in this trouble.'

'I agree, we gotta find the poor girl.'

Morgan stopped as a sudden thought hit him.

'Leo, can't you see, this Mex bandit you caught!' His eyes widened. 'It all ties in. He's brought his gang of cutthroats with him. He reckons to rustle Pentland cattle while your Cyrus Breen is distracted over his daughter's kidnapping. Whether he gets the ransom or not they'll head for the border once they have a big enough herd assembled. God knows what he'll do with the girl in that case.'

As if struck by the same thought the two lawmen turned and looked at their captive.

'I reckon this fella knows where they were meeting up

with the stolen cattle. My guess is that's where Ignacio will be and also your girlfriend.'

The Mexican stared back at them sullenly.

'I tell you I am innocent *vaquero* on my lawful business. I know nothing about no kidnapped girl and what did you say that fella's name was – Igor or what? Never heard of him.'

Sheriff Phil Morgan was staring speculatively at the prisoner. He began to wind the rope around the Mexican and draw it tight.

'You fellas look the other way. This ain't gonna to be pretty.'

'What you aim to do, Phil?'

Sheriff Morgan stared evenly at his partner.

'I'm gonna beat the information outa that piece of shit who reckons he don't know nothing.'

'Phil, we supposed to be on the side of law and order. What kinda lawman beats up on prisoners?'

'I never cottoned to Tom Grover and his sidekick Aidan Perry, but I sure as hell felt real bad at what happened to them. No man, no matter how obnoxious, deserved that kinda death. Think on that girl of yours in the hands of a sadistic thug like Ignacio. Now if you and Broderick look away you can't testify you saw me beat this man to a pulp.'

His intended victim hawked and spat. A gob of spittle landed on the sheriffs coat.

'Gringo pig dog! I tell you nothing.'

With a curiously nonchalant motion Sheriff Phil Morgan drove the butt of his Winchester into the bridge of the Mexican's nose. The man had been sitting on the ground glaring hatred at his captors. Suddenly he found himself stretched out in the dust in the most excruciating pain. He screamed and the lawman pushed the barrel of the rifle into the open mouth.

Blood was blocking his smashed nasal passages and the steel barrel jammed halfway down his throat was restricting air going in that way. He was wriggling frantically in a desperate attempt to breathe – his rowels scoring deep gouges in the earth. Even when the lawman removed the rifle from the bandit's mouth it was several minutes before he had recovered sufficiently to continue the interrogation.

'Now my friend, you are going to tell me where Ignacio is or your bones will be bleaching on this damn prairie. But I promise you one thing, it will be a slow and painful passing for you.'

'All right . . . I tell you . . . then you let me go. . . !'

## 28

Broderick rode into the yard at Pentland trailing the captured bandit on his horse. The outlaw was slumped atop the mount with hands and feet tethered. Behind him the rest of his crew dismounted and waited while the cowboy tied up his mount and walked up to the entrance of the ranch house and hammered on the door. Within minutes, a haggard-faced Cyrus Breen opened the door to him.

'Any news, Broderick?'

As the ranch owner spoke, Mrs McQueen pushed past him.

'Oh, tell us some good news, Broderick. We are out of our minds with worry. Poor Imogen, what must she be going through!'

'I have news, some of it good and some bad.'

The cowboy indicated the bandit still tied to his mount.

'We came upon a bunch of rustlers and managed to capture this one. He's part of the same gang as is holding Imogen to ransom. A couple of fellas riding through helped us. They persuaded this fella to tell them where the gang are holing up. Now they've gone on to the rustler's hideout. They told us to gather as many men as we can and follow after them.'

'What!' Cyrus exploded, 'I'm raising the goddamn money to pay the ransom. We still got a few days yet. These fellas are liable to blow the whole operation. I want my daughter back safe. Them fellas go blundering in they're liable to put Imogen' s life in danger.'

'They seemed to know the bandit as has corralled Imogen. They run across him afore. Mean *hombre* name of Ignacio. He's a real bad 'un. Killed a couple of US Marshals and stole their identity. It was him what fooled Miss Imogen, posing as a marshal. Somehow this Ignacio lured her to some place he could snatch her.'

'Did you come across any sign of Claude?' Victoria McQueen broke in anxiously.

'No, ma'am, I ain't seen him since this thing started. He's maybe in Ladler taking a break from all the worry.'

Victoria McQueen's face was lined with anxiety. Claude had ridden out to hijack the lawman's operation. His task was to get his hands on the money Imogen was 'borrowing' and somehow place the blame on the marshal. Since then, there had been no word of her errant son.

When the ransom note had arrived she had believed it was a crafty scheme on the part of Claude to get his hands on a lot more than the ten thousand Imogen had taken from her father's safe. She had rejoiced at the cleverness of it all.

Now she did not know what to think. If what Broderick

said was true then something had gone awry and Claude – who should have contacted her before now – might even be held captive along with Imogen.

She took very little notice of the feverish activity going on around her. Cowboys were rushing about saddling horses while Cyrus Breen was supervising the issue of arms to all the riders. The captured bandit was locked in a storeroom with his hands and feet bound. In all that time Victoria McQueen fretted and thought about nothing except the fate of her beloved son.

'Victoria.' Cyrus Breen had taken the woman to one side. 'I'm leading the men after this bandit, Ignacio. I fear for Imogen's safety if those fellas go stirring things up. It means it's up to me to rescue something from this fiasco. Why in the hell those strangers couldn't leave things alone as in no business of theirs? Another couple of days and I would have had the money gathered. Anyway I'm leaving you in charge of things here in case something new develops. Claude might come back with some news of Imogen or even Imogen herself, though I have little hope of that.'

'Yes, Cyrus, it's a bad time for us both with our children missing. But don't worry about this end of things, I'll take care of affairs here. Just you bring Imogen back home safe.'

They embraced briefly and then Cyrus rode out at the head of his men on his rescue mission.

Victoria McQueen watched the riders leave, a frown furrowing her handsome brow. Her feverish brain was working overtime. She bit her lip as she pondered her options. Her priority was to locate Claude. She had sent him out after eavesdropping on the bogus lawman as Imogen and he made their plans. Her problem was she was not sure of the location of the abandoned farm Imogen had used for the rendezvous. Claude had known of the place. He had ridden to town and hired men to go with him. Suddenly she came to a decision.

With decisive steps she went inside the house and, a while later, appeared with a pistol strapped around her ample hips. She unlocked the storeroom and peered in at the unprepossessing creature sitting on the floor leaning against a cupboard with his hands and feet bound.

'Right, my man, I have a little job for you. If you do it well I shall reward you with your freedom.'

The captive's look was mean and wicked as he eyed up the female. His gaze took in her generous bosom and travelled down the rest of her body, his eyes glinting as he assessed her. Victoria ignored his lustful gawking. She was well used to men eyeing up her charms.

'*Si*, I will help the beautiful *señora*. She has but to ask and I am her slave.'

'You know where this Ignacio met the young woman he took hostage? Well, I need you to take me there.'

The bandit's eyes became hooded as he considered the woman's words. He wondered if it was some trick to make him confess he was part of Ignacio's gang.

'When I was in town I overheard some men discussing this Ignacio. They did mention some plan involving a farm. Purely by chance I know where it is. I could take you there if you will release me.'

Victoria took out a clasp knife and sawed at the rope binding the man's ankles. She stepped briskly back and drew her pistol.

'Right, you come outside slowly. I warn you I can use this gun. You behave and take me to this farm. After that you're free to ride away. I just hope I never have to see your ugly face again.'

'*Si, señora*, I am vamoose from this terrible country

where innocent men are abused. I will serve the beautiful lady most faithfully.'

# 29

'More coffee, miss?'

Imogen looked askance at her host. She had been getting more and more worried at the absence of Leo. Surely by now he would have reappeared. She had urged Ignacio to go in search of the young lawman. But Ignacio asserted that Leo was engaged in a dangerous undercover game that could not be jeopardized by any premature action on their part.

She was concerned also about her prolonged stay at the lawmen's camp. There again Ignacio had reassured her that he had sent a note to her father telling him she was safe and would return home shortly. On top of these worries was the presence of so many villainous characters coming and going to the camp.

'It is necessary for Leo and myself to work with such men. They are part of our cover as stockmen who are not bothered by the legitimacy of any business deals.'

Ignacio had spread his hands expressively and shrugged his shoulders.

'You know how these things work. The men we are attempting to trap are suspicious of everyone. If they suspected we were not what we seem they would not hesitate to use extreme violence.'

'Nevertheless I have stayed much longer than I've ever been away from home. I must return today.'

'Impossible. I cannot afford an escort and I will not allow you to travel alone. I will not put your safety in jeopardy. Look what happened when that Claude McQueen attacked you.'

Imogen's patience snapped.

'Just give me a gun and I'll take my chances.'

Ignacio threw back his handsome, leonine head and laughed.

'You know I admire your spirit, but Leo would never forgive me if I let anything happened to you. You'll just have to wait for Leo.'

Imogen glared back at him; her large brown eyes, usually so soft, had now lost some of their gentleness. Before she could reply, one of the villainous-looking *vaqueros* whose presence had bothered her appeared beside Ignacio. The exchange was in rapid Spanish and some instinct prevented her from letting on that she could understand every word. The gist of her eavesdropping left her more uneasy than ever. Imogen was beginning to suspect that all was not as it seemed in the camp of this Marshal Grover.

According to the messenger two lawmen were approaching. The *vaquero* wanted to know if they were to be ambushed and killed or merely to be captured.

'What was all that about?' Imogen asked innocently.

'Things are coming along nicely. The men we are after have fallen into our trap. I want you out of the way while we deal with them. They are notorious gunmen and must be handled with great care. If you would stay in the cabin until this is over I would not have to worry about your safety. Pedro will stand guard outside and watch out for you.'

Ignacio spewed out instructions to Pedro. Imogen was to be kept inside for now. She was not to be allowed out under any circumstances until Ignacio himself had authorized it.

She watched the marshal leave and wondered why he had lied to her. As her suspicions mounted she began to make plans to slip away from the lawman and make her way home. First she would have to steal a weapon and she knew exactly where to obtain one. She had observed Ignacio place the gun he had taken from Claude inside the saddle-bags containing the ten thousand she had agreed to borrow for him and Leo.

'*Señorita.*'

Pedro indicated the door of the small cabin around which the camp had been organized. Imogen smiled sweetly and walked inside. Once the door was shut behind her she soon unearthed the saddle-bags from beneath a heap of buffalo robes. The money was there but the gun had disappeared.

'Damn!'

Imogen seldom swore but felt her disappointment required an outlet.

The small window at the rear of the cabin was too small to be of much practical use except for ventilation. A piece of sacking had been nailed across the frame. It was not difficult for Imogen to rip this covering away. Firstly she pushed the saddle-bags outside then tried to follow. This was more difficult than she had imagined and partway out she stuck. With some more swearing and after collecting a skinned knee and a bruised elbow she finally admitted defeat. Despondently she sat down and pondered her next move.

Cautiously taking a roundabout route the two lawmen approached the series of draws the captured rustler had told them about. Leo, having been raised in this part of the country, knew exactly what they were looking for.

'There's a whole series of draws running from east to

west,' he informed his companion. 'From what that rustler told us they're gathering the cattle in the main channel and when Ignacio gives the word they'll drive them south.'

He shook his head in annoyance.

'Broderick says the ransom note asked for fifty thousand dollars. If Cyrus pays up and loses all those cattle as well it'll about finish him. He ain't a young man anymore. I can't see him recovering from this much trouble. It'll mean starting from scratch again.'

'Yeah,' his companion agreed. 'You gotta hand it to Ignacio, he sure is one clever bastard. If he gets away with this dodge he'll be set up for a long time to come. He won't need to go robbing banks no more. He could even set up his own ranch with all those stolen cattle.'

'Hell, he could have it all just so long as I can get Imogen back safe. If he's as much as harmed a hair on her head I'll make him pay. What you did to that rustler back there will be nothing to what I'll do to him when I catch up with him.'

'How do you reckon on playing this hand, Leo? To round up all those steers Ignacio's bound to have a large crew with him. Maybe you haven't noticed, but there's just two of us.'

The two lawmen mulled over the problem for a while as they proceeded towards the area of broken hills and basins where they knew Ignacio had holed up.

'They're bound to have camp-fires and such. We'll spot their campsite and sneak in and assay the situation. If we could find out where Ignacio is holding Imogen we could maybe grab her and bust our way out again.'

'Post Mortem, with all that's happened since you joined up with the law I almost believe you could do just that. In the absence of any other ideas I guess we're stuck with that. Lay on, MacDuff.'

They spotted the smoke at the same time and reined in.

'I say we leave the horses here and go the rest of the way on foot,' Leo offered. 'We'll climb that hogback and take stock.'

At the top of the ridge they crawled cautiously to the rim. It was as the rustler had said. In the wide valley below them large numbers of cattle could be seen. As they watched something glinted amongst the pine-covered far wall of the valley.

'Reckon that was the refection off a rifle barrel,' Leo grunted. 'They'll have guards posted all around. Goddamn it, we move anywhere in that valley and we'll be spotted for sure.'

He squinted at the far end of the valley. From where they squatted they could see the drifting smoke from a wood fire but were unable to see anything within the pines.

'I guess there's nothing else for it, we'll have to sneak up there through the trees.'

They began the tedious crawling that they hoped would put them in a position to look down on the rustlers' camp. Before the lawmen got to their objective they came to the end of the tree cover.

'Goddamn it, Phil, we'll have to angle down and get among those steers and then make our way towards that grove of trees. It's from behind there the smoke is coming.'

Sweating in the intense heat that was being channelled down into the valley the two men crawled down to the bottom and began cautiously to thread their way through the steers. The heat that was causing the men to sweat was making the cattle docile. Two men on foot did nothing to alarm them.

Leo began herding a group of steers towards the trees

in an effort to cover their advance. The ruse seemed to be working for no one challenged them.

Once among the trees Leo drew his Colt and his companion did the same. Silently they went forward.

The camp was a temporary affair with tarpaulins rigged from the trees to provide shelter. A lone man sat at a fire with a long branch in his hand. A biscuit was speared on the end and he seemed totally engrossed in toasting this. There was no sign of anyone else about. Leo stood up straight and training his Colt on the lone man stepped out from the shelter of the trees.

The small noise he made attracted the man's attention and he turned his head and gazed directly at Leo. The scarred, tanned face that Leo remembered so well, creased in a smile.

'Deputy Postlewaite, what a surprise! Why don't you set and join me in a toasted biscuit?'

'Ignacio!'

Leo's gun was trained on the bandit leader. His finger ached on the trigger but yet he hesitated. This just seemed too easy.

'I see Sheriff Morgan is with you,' Ignacio continued blithely. 'It seems a long way from home. Are you on vacation?

'I'll ask my men to join the party.'

Leo stared in some consternation as the trees erupted with activity. Bandit after bandit stepped out from the trees. There were too many to count. All were holding weapons – either carbines or pistols. Leo cast a sideways glance at Morgan. The lawman was as much at a loss as he was. He shrugged and gave Leo a wry grin.

'Now if I was back in Denton sitting in on a poker game in the Silver Penny I would say this is a good time to start bluffing and tell this sonofabitch about the posse we got surrounding the camp.'

Ignacio laughed.

'You got two choices, my friends. You can die right now with several pounds of lead inside you or you can surrender your weapons and throw yourselves on my mercy.'

'Is that the same mercy you showed Marshals Tom Grover and Aidan Perry?' Sheriff Morgan asked.

Ignacio pulled the bread from the fire and critically examined it.

'Those pigs abused me when they thought they had me helpless. They deserved what they got. The injuries you gave me were suffered in a fair fight. We fought on equal terms and you won. Now it is my turn to detain you and then decide your fate.'

There was a noise behind the two lawmen. They did not need to turn around to know more bandits had crept in behind them. Leo watched with impotent rage as Ignacio speared another biscuit and turned his attention to the fire.

'My men are very nervous. At the first sign you want to resist they will blast you into oblivion. They have their instructions.'

'Where is Imogen?'

'Ah, the lovely Imogen – she is waiting to greet you. She has been waiting for her knight in shining armour to come to her rescue. I am pleased there is some romance left in the world.'

Ignacio made a signal to one of the waiting bandits.

'As soon as Deputy Postlewaite and Sheriff Morgan put down their weapons bring out the girl. If they resist, kill her.'

# 30

Leo glanced at Phil Morgan. The sheriff gave a slow smile.

'Your play, Post Mortem – we can kill the sonabitch and get killed ourselves, or surrender and die slow just like Tom Grover and Aidan Perry.'

'Goddamn it, Phil, that's a helluva thing to say at time like this. He's holding Imogen as his ace. It's time to fold.'

To Leo's surprise his companion tossed his Colt into the clearing.

'Someone said once, where's there's life there's hope.'

Leo's Colt followed the sheriff's onto the turf.

'Pedro, bring out our guest.'

The bandit thus addressed turned and kicked open the door of a dilapidated cabin.

'Come out, *señorita*, we have guests.'

The slight figure of Imogen appeared in the doorway of the cabin.

'Imogen.'

Leo made to step forward. Ignacio made a quick sign to his men.

'Take them.'

As he was grabbed from behind Leo saw Imogen struggling between two burly outlaws.

'Leo,' she called.

But Leo was helpless as rough hands pushed the lawmen into the clearing. There was the sound of a scuffle and a yell of defiance from Imogen.

'Perfect. My victory is complete. You can have a grandstand seat while your erstwhile boyfriend bares all before you.

'Tie her to a tree and make sure she is secure.'

'Leo. . . !'

Leo watched helplessly as Ignacio's men secured the girl to the tree – pulling callously on the rope so that it bit cruelly into her body. Her eyes never left the young lawman lying by the fire.

'I love you, Leo,' she called.

'How touching. I'm sure Leo returns the sentiment. Watch while he bleeds for you.'

The bandits were efficient. In a short time they had the helpless lawmen tied hands and wrists on each side of the fire. It was a humiliating and uncomfortable position for them both.

'You got any ideas, Post Mortem?'

Leo pursed his lips as if he was thinking over the problem.

'We could try calling for help.'

A shadow fell across Leo as the bandit chief moved alongside him. In his hand was a soft leather roll. He set this on the ground and unfolded the bundle. Leo stared at the row of knives stored inside the leather, each in its own individual pocket.

The bandit extracted a knife with a short flat blade. He gently ran this along the buttons of Leo's shirt. The garment fell open as the threads parted with no pull on the razor edge.

'I always start on the upper body. When you are begging me to kill you I shall remove the lower garments and perform more delicate surgery. It takes a long time. I hope you had no urgent appointments. This is my skinning knife. You'll like my skill with this.'

'Go to hell, you sick bastard!'

Ignacio grinned and, reaching out, began to work. Leo gritted his teeth. No sound came from his lips as the knife began its grisly work. In the background he could hear Imogen sobbing.

'Sonabitch,' Leo snarled defiantly through the pain. 'I'm gonna get you for this.'

Before he could continue there was a flurry of gunfire somewhere down in the valley. The bandit leader looked surprised. He looked at the two lawmen.

'You brung reinforcements?' he queried.

'Sure thing,' drawled Morgan. 'There's a posse surrounding this here valley. No matter what you do to us you'll never get away from here.'

For one terrible moment the bandit chief raised the knife as if he was about to plunge it into his young victim. The lawmen could see the desire to kill in the bandit's eyes.

'You can wait. I will deal with these foolish men who go against Ignacio and then I shall come back and finish with you. Don't bleed to death while you wait for me.'

Turning to his men he issued instructions. In a short time the clearing was empty of bandits. Leo turned his head and stared over at Imogen.

'I love you too, Imogen. When we get outa this mess I'm gonna marry you no matter what Cyrus says.'

'Oh, my poor Leo, you're bleeding so. I know it's all my fault you're here. I know you came to rescue me. I'm sorry.'

'Sorry? There's nothing to be sorry about. I was coming back for you anyhow and then we ran into this trouble.'

'Howdy, miss, I'm Phil Morgan seeing as how this deputy of mine won't introduce us.' The sheriff's laconic voice interrupted the exchange between the young lovers. 'I take it you're the young woman this fella has been mooning over ever since I met him.'

'Sorry, Phil, I guess this ain't the best of circumstances

to introduce my future bride.'

'That's all right, kid. How are you holding up?'

'It's hellish painful but I don't think he's done too much damage yet. The bastard . . . sorry, Imogen . . . he ain't had time to do me any serious injury. Peeled some skin off my chest and belly. But we gotta get out of this afore he returns.'

As he was talking Leo had been wriggling around. He was looking speculatively at the fire. Without saying a word to his friends he began to manoeuvre closer to the fire.

'Leo, you're mighty close to them there coals,' warned Morgan.

Leo almost cried out as the flames licked at his arms.

'Guide me, Phil. I'm gonna burn these goddamn ropes off me.'

And then he could not suppress a groan as the flames took hold.

'Leo. . . !'

The clearing was filled with the smell of burning rawhide and charred flesh. The young lawman writhed beside the fire unable to suppress his groans as the fire bit into his arms. Imogen sobbed piteously as she saw what was happening to the man she loved.

As the agony in Leo's roasted arms increased so also it seemed that the pain of the wounds inflicted by Ignacio became excruciating. In getting his wrists into position at the fire he had inadvertently rolled on his front and dirt and ashes had ground into the raw flesh. A terrible urge to scream rose in him as the agony in his body became unbearable. He could taste blood in his mouth where he had bitten his tongue and lips to keep from yelling out loud. But he forced down the terrible screams rising up in him because Imogen, his girl, was watching his ordeal.

146

Pride as well as a stubborn desire to bring the outlaw chief to justice kept his arms in the searing heat of the flames.

Finally he could no longer stand the dreadful torment his body was suffering. With an audible groan he rolled away from the flames. He wondered which was the worse agony as the raw wounds in his chest and stomach rubbed over the coarse earth and more dirt and grit were ground into his suffering flesh.

For moments he lay as still as he was able, hoping to keep the pain in his body from growing worse. He was almost sobbing as he struggled for breath. His mind wanted to disconnect and black out. Desperately he willed himself to ignore the pain.

'Oh, Leo. . . .'

He could hear Imogen sobbing as she watched him suffer.

Gathering his reserves of strength and determination he tensed his arms. Fresh agony lanced through the tortured limbs. Slowly he forced his wrists against his restraints. He was certain the scorched rawhide was biting through the seared flesh of his wrists and cutting into the bone. A sudden scream of frustration and agony was torn from his lungs as he made one last supreme effort to burst the weakened bonds. And then his tortured body could take no more and darkness swamped over him.

## 31

*'Goddamn you son, I'm gonna flay the flesh from your bones!'*
'Cyrus, I never touched Imogen! I love her. . . .'

The bullwhip snaked out and slashed across his chest. A piece of his flesh came away where the rawhide thong bit. Leo screamed that he was innocent but Cyrus was not listening.

'I'll teach you to meddle with my daughter.'

The pain was unbearable.

'I love her,' he whispered

Imogen was calling him now. He could hear her voice as he tensed for the next blow of the whip.

'Leo . . . please, Leo, wake up . . . oh please, Leo . . .' Her voice dissolved into a sob. 'Leo . . . Leo. . . .'

She was weeping for him. He forced his eyes open. His body was on fire. He needed a river to drown in – a cool-running, clear river where he could see the bottom. He could drift along with the fallen leaves. . . .

'Goddamn it, Leo, get off your goddamn ass and do something!'

He thought he knew that voice.

'Phil,' he croaked, 'where the hell are you?'

'Here, you goddamn fool!'

'Leo . . . oh thank God, Leo . . . I thought you were dead.'

He certainly knew that voice.

'Imogen . . . is that you. . . ?'

Along with the pain came memory. He rolled over and wished he had stayed still. There was so much agony in his charred arms. His chest was a weeping sore. He forced himself to his hands and knees. The burnt ropes that had held him lay beside the fire. So much pain and agony in order to burn them through and free his hands.

Slowly he stood. Swaying on his feet he looked across at Imogen. She was staring at him with something akin to horror in her eyes.

'Oh, my poor Leo, look what they've done to you!'

'Don't cry,' he said foolishly, and stepped towards her.

His foot caught on a snag. He looked down and saw the rolled up leather bundle. The knives that Ignacio had used to flay him! His hands were trembling as he fumbled with the straps. His fingers and wrists were blackened bits of burnt charcoal. Every movement was a searing effort of pain. He staggered over to Imogen. His attempt at a grin was more like a grimace of agony.

He sawed at the rope. His charred fingers just about held the knife. The rawhide rope parted under the razor edge like rotten cotton. As the rope dropped away Imogen threw her arms around Leo. He held his arms out from his sides unable to embrace her because of the pain.

'When you two lovers can spare the time I'd like a little help here,' Sheriff Morgan called laconically.

Reluctantly Imogen released Leo.

'Get a knife from the bag there,' Leo told her. 'I'll look around for weapons.'

Her blouse was stained with the blood from his weeping wounds. Leo stuck the skinning knife into his belt and forced himself to walk to the cabin. He meant to step inside but the effort was too much for his weakened state and he sprawled instead.

'Hell, Post Mortem, no time for that now, we gotta get outa here.'

With some difficulty, Leo sat up blinking foolishly at Sheriff Morgan.

'I figured to look for weapons.'

'Well, by a strange oversight they left our Colts right where we tossed them. I guess they thought we wouldn't be needing them anymore.'

Morgan stepped gingerly around Leo and gently helped him to his feet.

'Let's get some dressings on those wounds. I declare in my career as a lawman I never patched up a fella so much as you. Knives and you just don't mix. Come to think of it, fires would come a close second.'

Leo was in too much pain to think of a suitable reply.

They rummaged amongst the belongings of the gang and found bandages. Inside the old cabin Imogen remembered seeing bottles of rotgut. Not asking permission, Morgan poured a generous amount on to the wounds on Leo's body.

'Goddamn you, Phil,' he groaned, as the agony of his wounds increased a hundredfold with the administration of the raw liquor. 'I think I'd rather have Ignacio work on me as you.'

Leo snatched the bottle from his partner and upended it into his mouth. As the fire inside him began to spread, the fire in his wounds lessened slightly.

Imogen took over then and began the tedious task of binding up his fire-ravaged arms. As she worked she told him how she had come to be in the bandits' camp.

As they tended to Leo's injuries they became aware of the shooting war still going on. The firing was continuous.

'Someone sure is catching hell,' Morgan remarked wryly.

Leo, lost in his own agony, suddenly stared at Imogen.

'Cyrus! I bet that's your pa with the Pentland crew being attacked. I sent Broderick back with a prisoner and told him to round up a crew to follow us in here.'

He looked at his partner.

'We gotta help. Cyrus will have his crew from the ranch. They're cowhands not gunfighters. Ignacio's men are well armed and used to this sort of fighting. They'll slaughter those cowboys.'

Sheriff Morgan was frowning as he rubbed a hand across his face.

'Damn it, Leo, we need our rifles to take any effective action. They're back with the horses. I guess Ignacio is between us and our mounts.'

'There are plenty of weapons here,' Imogen interjected. 'Those bandits kept a store of rifles and pistols along with ammunition. It's back in the trees. I'll show you.'

'Lay on, Macduff,' Morgan said.

Leo raised a bandaged arm.

'I wish you wouldn't say that, Phil. The last time you did we walked into Ignacio's trap.'

Morgan stared speculatively at the youngster. He reminded the sheriff of nothing more than a butchered steer. Bloody bandages obscured the worst of the ravages. He cringed as he tried to imagine the pain of that damaged body.

'You stay here with Imogen, I'll fetch the weapons.' He looked at Leo's damaged hands.

'Will you manage a rifle with those hands? I don't think you'll be able to hold a Colt.'

The youngster's eyes were bleak as he gazed back at the lawman.

'I'll do whatever it takes. I ain't gone through all this to chicken out now.'

Morgan nodded and went in search of the guns. The two youngsters were alone.

'When this is all over, Imogen, will you come away with me? I've started a new life in Denton. Sheriff Morgan made me his deputy. It ain't much but at least we would be together. But maybe it's asking too much of you to leave Pentland and all the comforts there. I know it was a wrench for me to leave. . . .'

He could say no more for his face was held in her hands and she was kissing him.

151

'Leo Postlewaite, wherever you go, there go I.'

They broke apart only when Morgan returned.

Bandoleers crisscrossed his chest and three Remington rifles were slung on his shoulders.

'I'll carry your weapon, Leo.'

Morgan looked questioningly at Imogen.

'Can you fire one of these?'

Her smile was forced as she answered.

'Pa taught me to shoot a rifle and ride a horse. Sometimes I wonder if he wished at times I were a boy and not a girl. Leo here took the place of a son until he ran foul of Pa.'

Morgan handed her one of the rifles.

'Let's do it then.'

## 32

'Looks like they got our boys pinned down.'

The bandits had good cover amongst the pine trees of the valley slope. The three refugees had come up behind the ambushers and now could see them clearly as they crouched amongst the trees and fired down on the trapped cowboys.

Morgan handed Leo a rifle. The youngster cradled it in his arms and forced his injured finger into the trigger guard.

'Now listen up you two,' the older lawman spoke quietly to his companions. 'You've seen what these men are capable of. You only have to look at Leo to realize what kind of beasts we are dealing with. They're intent on murdering those men down in the valley bottom. Their only hope is us three up here. What I'm trying to say is, we can show them no mercy. Just point that rifle and imagine you are shooting vermin. Every one of those bandits you gun down saves the life of one of your friends. Now pick a spot and start firing when I give the signal.'

Leo crouched down behind a fallen tree trunk and rested the rifle on it. The bandages that draped his body were soaked with blood and sweat. His hands and arms felt as if they were still plunged into the flames. Tremors of pain racked him.

To his right he could see Imogen kneeling behind the bole of a large pine. Somewhere off to his left Morgan was setting himself. Leo squinted down the rifle barrel and sighted on a bandit wearing a red shirt.

On the trail below could be seen the bodies of two cowboys. A horse had also been killed and it sprawled dark and ominous on the earth. The Pentland crew were pinned down and could neither move backward nor forward. Even as he watched another was hit and he could see the man pitch to the ground.

'Let the shooting commence,' called Morgan.

Leo squeezed the trigger and saw his target jerk and crumble out of sight. On either side his companions opened up. They fired and fired into the gang of ambushers. The bandits were scrambling about in an attempt to find cover from this unexpected attack. In a short time two more men measured their length among the pine needles.

The cowboys trapped in the valley floor realized something unusual was happening for they increased their fire against the bandits.

It was a complete reversal of fortunes. Now the ambushers were being shot at from both directions and it was having an effect on their own ability to return fire. They were torn between shooting down at the cowboys or firing up at these fresh attackers.

Some bullets came uphill to the three rifles but the firing was sporadic and inaccurate. Leo and his party were too well hidden in the trees to give a clear shot to anyone.

It brought panic and confusion amongst the bandits. No matter which way they turned they were being fired upon. It could not last. As more and more of their companions were killed or wounded suddenly the bandits broke and ran.

Men were clambering through the trees in all directions. The three rifles in the trees above them poured a relentless hail of fire at the fleeing gunmen. Between them they shot at anything that moved and there were certainly plenty of targets to shoot at. Any movement in the trees was an invitation to the three sharpshooters.

The bandits were in a panic now, calling out to the riflemen to cease shooting. Some were putting hands up over their heads and yelling they wanted to give up. A few plucked kerchiefs and waved them from behind trees in the hope that it would spare them from the deadly hail of lead coming at them from both directions. Slowly the firing petered out.

'Stay under cover,' Morgan ordered his companions, then began to yell instructions to the bandits. 'Throw out your weapons and put your hands up in the air. Anyone not obeying will be shot. Either of you know any Spanish?' he queried.

'I do,' answered Imogen.

'Just go over what I've told them. Yell it down at them.'

Imogen repeated Morgan's instructions. Below them men were stepping into the open with upraised hands. Morgan stood up. He was gesturing to the bandits to move well away from their discarded weapons when from behind a gun blasted and the lawman stumbled forward and collapsed on to his face. Leo was turning when something smashed into his temple. He slumped over the tree trunk he had been using as a rifle rest. His senses swam and he desperately tried to push himself upright. He heard Imogen scream. His head felt as if it was cracked open and blood was pouring down the side of his face.

He tried to swing round. There was a scuffle from nearby and another scream. He slumped back and stared at the place where Imogen had crouched just seconds before. In an agonizing dilemma he turned to look for Morgan. The sheriff was upright again and though he was sitting on the ground he still had his rifle trained on the bandits. They seemed unaware that the odds had changed in their favour and then it did not matter. The Pentland cowboys were swarming up the hillside with weapons trained on the disarmed bandits.

Leo lurched to his feet. He had a fair idea what had happened. Somehow Ignacio had gotten behind them, shot Morgan and buffaloed him.

Clasping the Remington to his ruined chest with hands that were an inferno of agony Leo stumbled up the hillside. He reckoned the bandit chief would race back to the cabin hoping to rescue the saddle-bag of money. With Imogen as hostage he could grab a horse and ride to freedom.

The clearing in front of the shack was empty. Unsure of where the bandit's remuda was, Leo hesitated.

Sweat and blood was making the front of his body slippery. His whole being was an inferno of pain. Impotently he staggered into the clearing. Then he heard the horses. He brought up his rifle and stared into the trees.

They were coming fast – Ignacio in front and leading a

horse. Imogen's frail form was slumped on top of the second horse.

'Ignacio, that's as far as you go!'

The spurs dug in and the bandit's horse leapt forward. Straight at Leo they came – horse and rider bearing down on the bloodied figure swaying in the middle of the clearing. Leo triggered and knew he had missed. He flung himself to one side and the horse thundered down on him.

The scream was torn from him as he hit the ground. Pain and dizziness swept over him as his tortured body rolled on the rough ground. He was vaguely aware of the horse screaming along with him. Then horse and rider were tumbling on to the earth and he realized his shot had not missed.

The horse was still screaming as it thrashed around on the ground. Blood was pouring from the bullet hole in the animal's chest. But Leo did not have time to worry about the horse. The man who had been thrown from the horse was climbing to his feet and grabbing for a pistol. The holster was empty and with a scream of rage the bandit leader hurled himself at the young cowboy as he came off the ground.

Leo had no time to defend himself as the bandit crashed into him. He went down under the impact. A fist in his face dazed him momentarily. Ignacio was wrestling the rifle from Leo's grasp. It was no contest. Leo's hands were so damaged he was unable to hold on to it. The roasted skin on his hands came away with the rifle. Helplessly he dropped his hands as the rifle was reversed and the muzzle was pressed into his face.

'You goddamn jinx. Every time I come up against you, things go wrong. Well this is the end, lawman. I should have killed you instead of waiting. You've dogged my steps

156

for the last time. I'm tempted to let you live so you can picture me and your girl living it up somewhere. But I've messed around with you for too long.'

Leo was feebly scrabbling with his burnt hands trying to push Ignacio from him. His damaged fingers touched the haft of the knife he had taken from Ignacio's pouch of knives. The skin on his fingers was almost non-existent. He could feel the blood and mucus weeping from the burned digits and making his hands slippery.

'The law will catch up with you, Ignacio. You'll swing as was intended.'

The knife came free as Ignacio jacked a shell into the rifle. The round muzzle of the weapon was pressed into Leo's forehead.

'Goodbye, lawman . . . I only wish I had time to finish the skinning job I started on you.'

With one supreme effort Leo drove the knife up into the soft tissue of the bandit chief's neck. It took little effort on his part for the razor-sharp blade to scythe a hole into the bandit's throat. Desperately Leo twisted and worked the blade up inside the neck.

Gouts of blood erupted from the terrible wound opening up in the throat. It splashed onto the youngster's already saturated front. The rifle slid to one side. Ignacio opened his mouth as if to protest this cruel blow. More blood dribbled from suddenly insensible lips. The body leaned forward and with horrible gagging noises the bandit chief gently subsided onto Leo.

The youngster struggled to move the dead weight crushing down upon him but his strength spent, he was much too weak to push the dead man from him. He tried to call out but his throat was dry. Leo closed his eyes and the world went peaceful in a blissful wave of darkness.

## 33

It was the jolting of the moving vehicle that brought him around. There were vague memories of being lifted and moved about and voices calling him. He was reluctant to surface again. Pain was a constant rasping at the raw ache that was his body.

The first thing he saw was the canvas covering of the wagon he was travelling in. Then a face was bending over him.

'Imogen. . . !'

'Leo, don't worry. I'm here to look after you. I'm never going to let you out of my sight ever again.'

He smiled and allowed his eyes to soak up the exquisite vision of the girl he loved.

'You are the loveliest girl in the whole of Texas. I'm a lucky man.'

Her lips came down on him. When she released him they gazed at each other content to be together at last.

'I still got to face your pa. I ain't looking forward to that.'

There was a mischievous twist to her smile.

'Pa,' she called, 'someone here's asking for you.'

A head poked inside from the driving seat of the wagon. There was a broad smile on the face of Cyrus Breen.

'Welcome home, son, and thanks for all you done to save Imogen.'

'Cyrus . . . I . . . thanks . . . I. . . .'

Leo was lost for words as he gazed at the man he had always regarded as his father.

The rancher's smile broadened.

'There's someone else here wants to say hello.'

The skirt was pulled back all the way and Leo saw his friend, Phil Morgan twisting round to peer at him. He could see the bandage on the lawman's shoulder.

'How are you, Phil?'

'Aw, just a hole on the shoulder. When I saw you and that Ignacio hugging each other back there I thought you were both dead. You really took a liking to that fella.'

Leo had an almost irresistible impulse to laugh.

'He sure had a lump in his throat as we parted,' he said.

The curtain closed and Leo was alone with Imogen again. And then he remembered why Phil Morgan and he had come all the way to Pentland.

'Imogen, there's some more unpleasant work ahead. The reason Phil and I came here was to investigate Victoria McQueen.'

Her face clouded over.

'That's all been taken care of. When I told Pa all that happened he reckoned that Ignacio would not have informed the sheriff in Ladler as he said about Claude being at the farm. He said we would stop by the disused ranch where we met up and rescue him. Claude was there . . . as was his mother . . . they were both dead, Pa and Phil wouldn't let me go in. They're sending a wagon to take the bodies to Ladler for burial.'

Her hand crept into his. They were both silent after that. The wagon rumbled on.

'You still bent on going back to Denton as a lawman?'

He turned the question over in his mind before answering.

'I never really wanted to be a lawman. The only thing I ever wanted to be was a cowhand. You think in view of everything that's happened Cyrus would consider giving me a job at Pentland?'

'Leo Postlewaite, my husband is not going to be a common cowhand. If I have my way he'll be joint owner of Pentland along with his wife.'

Leo stared at her.

'You think Cyrus will agree to that?'

She had that mischievous grin on her face again. 'I told him that was the condition he would have to agree to if we were to return and live at Pentland.'

For a moment he gazed at her.

'Imogen Breen, that wouldn't be a proposal of marriage I heard just then.'

She leaned over him, her long dark hair caressing his face.

'You better believe it, Mr Postlewaite.'